D0288623

GAUCHO

BY

GLORIA GONZALEZ

*IN
LOVING MEMORY
OF
SARA DAWN PAULSON*
1975-1990

BULLSEYE BOOKS • ALFRED A. KNOPF

NEW YORK

1

Upstairs, behind him, loud Spanish music flew out the window and bounced on the sidewalk.

He could hear his family laughing and dancing, shouting and stomping. Hopefully someone would call the cops and tell them to break it up, but since it was 1:30 on a hot Sunday afternoon, Gaucho didn't believe any of the neighbors would complain.

Besides, all the neighbors were at the party.

"Gaucho. Gauchito," his mother called, leaning out the second-floor window.

He pretended not to hear and sat rigidly on the stoop, staring across the street.

"Gauchito. *Por favor.*" Her voice carried softly, with a tinge of sadness.

"Come up, *hijo*. We gonna cut the cake, and I wanna take your picture, in your new suit, to send to the family."

Gaucho stiffened his body and pressed his legs against

the cool edge of the cement steps. He knew if he turned around she'd discover he'd been crying. Even though he had stopped an hour ago, somehow she would still be able to tell, and then she'd get upset and lead an army of relatives down to determine the cause of his grief.

If he wanted to talk to any of them, he wouldn't be sitting on the stoop in ninety-five-degree heat, wearing a bulky new suit, tight shoes, and high socks. His tie was streaked with sweat where he'd used it to dab his face and neck.

"Por favor, Gauchito."

He hated when she called him that. It made him sound like a baby. He didn't mind it when he was sick and lying in bed and she'd rub his chest with medicine. That was all right. But here in the daytime, with the sun out and people in the street—he hated it.

Still . . . it hurt him to hear her sounding so sad— but not enough to get him to turn around and answer her. He stared at the sidewalk and counted the black pieces of bubblegum stuck on the pavement.

Down the block, the traffic was slowly winding its way out of the city toward the beaches of Long Island. Gaucho wished he had brought his portable radio with him, if for no other reason than to blot out the Spanish music. He couldn't understand how anybody could listen to that junk. The singers all sounded like they were gargling. He'd take the "Top Ten" anytime.

Gaucho casually turned around (as casual as one can

be when one is drowning in sweat), pretended to wave away a mosquito, and glanced up at the open window. His mother was gone. In her place were a couple of beer cans that someone had propped there to free his hands for dancing. If a Spanish person ever lost his hands, he wouldn't be able to dance.

He shrugged and dabbed at the sweat trickling down behind his ears. He knew it wouldn't be easy to run away, because he had nowhere to run to. All his family lived in Puerto Rico. His only relative living in New York was his uncle Pachecko, but he lived in the Bronx and Gaucho knew he would never be able to find it by himself. You had to take three subways and a bus. Not that Pachecko cared; he drove a brand-new Cadillac. He probably didn't know what a subway was.

Anyway, Gaucho couldn't run away to Pachecko's house because Pachecko was at the party.

"Damn! You sure is some kind of jerk!" said Mario.

Gaucho didn't bother to turn around. There was no mistaking Mario's fat voice. In school, the teacher constantly urged him to "exercise vocal restraint," and Mario always promised to try and always failed. "I can't help it. I got a big voice because everything about me is big," he would announce from the rear of the classroom.

They had been friends since Gaucho moved into their building on Manhattan's Upper West Side six years ago, when his family first came from Puerto Rico. Gaucho was five then, and Mario had been his first "American" friend. Except that Mario was also Puerto Rican, only he had been born in New York.

"Why you sitting out here like some jerk when they have all that food up there? You know what they got on your kitchen table? Cake, ice cream, soda, beer, black beans, pork, watermelon . . . You crazy as hell! You know that?"

Gaucho eyed him coldly. "Drop dead, creep."

Mario pushed a paper plate at him. It held a big piece of cake and a scoop of melting strawberry ice cream. "Your mama told me to bring it to you." He took a plastic fork from his pocket.

"You can take it right back."

"Like hell!" Mario said as he plopped down alongside Gaucho and began eating.

Gaucho got up and moved to the other end of the stoop. "You have to make so much noise when you eat?"

"Tough! This is my stoop, too. You don't own the building." Mario jabbed his tongue into the mound of ice cream.

Gaucho decided to ignore him and reached for a comic book from the stack next to him. The sun overhead plastered his clothes to his body, and the colored ink from the cartoon figures spread across his sweaty fingers. Surprisingly, his pants still had a crease down the leg, and he pinched the material to make it stand up straighter.

Gaucho always had to be doing two things at once.

Even when he was reading, his free hand would twist the medal of the Virgin Mary around his neck. Or he'd fool with his hair, or pick at a scab, or chew on the inside of his mouth. One thing he was proud of: for all his nervousness, he never once bit his nails. When he grew up he never wanted anyone to look at his hands and mark him as a poor person or a laborer. Uncle Pachecko had lectured him that a man's hands tell more than his voice. "You cannot change your voice, but you can change what your hands 'say,' " Pachecko had taught him.

Every Saturday morning without fail, Pachecko would go to the barbershop at the Statler Hilton Hotel on 33rd Street and get a manicure.

"Sure, it costs me money, but when I shake hands with a person, my hands tell that person, 'I have never done a day's labor,' " Gaucho remembered his uncle telling him.

Pachecko's philosophy was that the only part of the human body that should work is the brain. Everything else should be on a lifelong vacation.

"Where'd you get all them comics, huh?" Mario sucked the vanilla icing on the cake.

"Bought 'em. And don't talk to me when I'm reading, 'cause then I gotta go back and start from the beginning."

Mario finished eating and sailed the paper plate across

the street, almost hitting a woman wheeling a baby carriage. She looked up toward the roof. In this neighborhood, it was always safer to walk looking up.

Mario burped. "You never have any money to buy anything. You stole them comics!"

"Like hell!" Gaucho confronted him. "I got ten dollars this morning from *Tio* Pachecko, and I spent half of it at the candy store. If you don't believe me, go ask Pinky."

Pinky was old, white-haired, and stooped-over. His rosy complexion was due to his high blood pressure. His high blood pressure was due to his belief that every kid who walked into his store was there to rob him. Not that he actually ever caught anyone stealing, but he attributed that to his own unrelenting surveillance over the store. Imagine if he ever relaxed? They'd steal the stools from the soda fountain. That's why he had them bolted to the floor.

"Bull!" Mario thumbed through one of the comics. "You ain't even allowed to go to the candy store alone. I heard your mother tell my mother about all the junkies who hang out there, and she won't send you anymore to get the paper."

Gaucho yanked the comic out of Mario's hand. "Just because I ain't allowed don't mean I don't go. Get it?"

He went back to reading about Underwater Man, who was entangled in the green arms of a giant octopus with purple suction cups. Right behind him was a school of fish! And there, on top of the water, his shadow blotting out the sun, was that greatest menace of all—

"Gaucho! Get the hell up here. Move it!"

He let the book drop slowly to his lap and lowered his head.

"You hear me!"

Again, Gaucho didn't have to turn around. He knew his brother's voice.

"If you're not up here in two minutes, I'm coming after you!"

Mario pretended to be deeply involved in tying his sneakers. It was okay if he fought with Gaucho, but it upset him to hear someone else yell at him. He caught Gaucho's attention and gave him a quick nervous smile.

He remembered the day Gaucho moved into the building. It was winter and everything was covered with snow. Even the garbage cans and the fire hydrant.

Mario had been on the stoop throwing snowballs at cars when the taxi pulled up and deposited Gaucho, his mother, and Angel, his brother. Gaucho had been afraid to step on the snow and had to be carried. Mario thought it was pretty dumb and said so to his mother at dinner. She responded by immediately going to visit the new family. Within the hour they were all seated around Mario's kitchen table.

He and Gaucho were told to go in the living room to

play, which Mario did reluctantly. This new kid was too much of a sissy. So what if he had never seen snow before. Was it something to be scared of?

Mario had opened the window, scooped up a handful of the cold, wet snow, and shoved it down Gaucho's back.

Gaucho had reacted by punching Mario on the side of his head. His ear stung and throbbed like a red neon sign. It was at that moment that they became best friends—at age five.

"He sure sounds mad," Mario whispered.

"Yeah." Gaucho sighed.

The belt on his trousers formed a thick wet line across his body, but he'd melt into a puddle before he'd go upstairs and change. He looked down at his brand-new black patent-leather shoes with the thick white stitching. There was a smudge near the little toe, and he quickly rubbed it away to its former sheen. He would always love these particular shoes because he had picked them out himself in a shoe store and had been waited on by a salesman and been told by the cashier to "come back again."

Usually his shoes came in a Christmas basket with cans of food and a skinny chicken delivered by the woman from the welfare department.

It was a lot more fun to go to a store and pick out the shoes himself and have the man wrap them in white tissue paper, stick them in a box, and put the whole thing in a bright paper bag with the name of the store right across the side so that when he walked down the street and ran into one of the guys, he would know right away that Gaucho had been out spending money. Gaucho "happened" to run into almost everyone he knew that day.

"You can turn around. He's gone," Mario said, glancing up at the window.

Gaucho wished his friend would also disappear. He wasn't in the mood for talking . . . reading . . . fighting. He just wanted to be alone.

That's why he loved his room—if you could call it that—because he could be alone but yet not too alone. It wasn't even a real room. It used to be the kitchen pantry—a long, deep, dark closet that you walked into, which had a lot of shelves along the wall to store canned food. He and Mama had removed the shelves, except for the ones high up, near the ceiling, where he now kept his personal belongings. With the wooden shelves gone, there was just enough space to stick in a comfortable cot against the wall and a bureau and mirror at the rear of the tiny boxlike space. Since there wasn't any electric outlet in the former closet, Mama and Gaucho had removed the heavy door, which led to the kitchen, and replaced it with a thin, almost transparent floral drapery that allowed the kitchen light to filter in and make the room glow softly. The curtain also assured Gaucho of privacy. He and Mama had a silent understanding that when the curtain was drawn across the doorway, she would knock on the nearby wall or call out to him before entering.

So he had the best of both worlds, privacy without being isolated. At night, Mama would be in the kitchen cooking or ironing, humming to herself, while a few feet away Gaucho slept easily, lulled by the familiar sounds . . . water running from the faucet . . . the refrigerator buzzing . . . the pots clanging in the sink.

And long after he was supposed to be asleep, enough light would creep through his curtain from the kitchen so that he could read his comics or play quietly with his miniature cars while in bed.

However, Gaucho's favorite part of the kitchen was the bathtub. It was a deep, narrow sink connected to a second shallow sink used for dishes. When the tub wasn't in use, it was covered by a wide white porcelain cover where Mama kept the toaster and her smelly onion plant. (Mama used to "make" the plants by taking a fat onion, piercing it with toothpicks, and placing it half-submerged in a glass of water. Yellow-green roots would sprout in all directions and then burst out in leaves. It was pretty until you got close and smelled the onion water.)

For Gaucho, the great thing about taking a bath in the kitchen was that he could watch the television in the living room. Sometimes on cold nights he would sit in the hot water for over an hour playing with his soldiers and watching a movie.

He was in the second grade before he found out that bathtubs are not normally found in kitchens. Since all his friends lived in the same kind of apartment as he did, he figured everyone did. He found out differently when his class visited a museum that had a big display of dollhouses. Every house had a special room just for bathing. He couldn't wait to get home and tell Mama.

"Back home we always had a bathroom all by itself," Mama told him. "It's only here that people do things so strange. To tell you the truth, from the first day I got here, I never liked the bathtub in the kitchen."

Gaucho preferred it. Especially on a cold winter night when you'd step out of the water and stand near the oven. The only drawback was that you couldn't bathe when there was company. Wherever you sat in the apartment—which only consisted of the kitchen and living room—you could see the tub.

"Someday when we get money, we will move into a real apartment with a real bathroom." This was not the least of Mama's dreams.

"As long as it has a fire escape," Gaucho would answer. That was his other passion. On hot summer nights he would step out onto the fire escape and curl up on a mattress of pillows. The light from the street lamp below cast a soft glow on the red bricks of the buildings around him.

On really hot, humid, stifling nights, everyone slept on the roof. As many as fifteen families would spread their blankets out on the hot tar, which would still be warm and moist at midnight. The only fear about sleeping on the roof was that the battalion of pigeons would splatter you. You also ran the risk of returning to your apartment in the morning and finding it stripped clean.

But in the insufferable, suffocating, killing heat of a New York City heat wave, these were minor considerations.

The adults were fond of repeating, "It gets hot back home, but never like this." And then they would debate why and decide it was cooler in Puerto Rico because of the ocean breezes and the trees and the open spaces that allowed the wind to dance and stretch its fingers. "Here, the wind comes up against a brick wall and dies."

Mario coughed and cleared his throat. He nudged Gaucho. "Maybe you better go up. He really sounded mad."

Gaucho gazed across the street at a gang of pigeons that fluttered and wiggled on the ledge of the roof. Now and then a new traveler would arrive and bump another into the air.

The sun baked his cheeks as he stared at the roof.

"Okay! Sit there! Don't talk to me. But I think you're stupid as hell, man, to stay here not eating—not talking—sweating to death—with everybody mad at you. And for what! Just 'cause your brother got married today."

2

It wasn't so much that Angel—or "Angie," as the guys called him—got married; it was who he married.

Denise. Redheaded, freckled, white as a quart of milk, Denise Raddigan. She was a stark contrast to Angel, with his dark skin and tight, wiry hair. Together they looked like an ad for vanilla and chocolate ice cream cones.

They had met in front of Radio City Music Hall when Denise's car stalled and conked out. It was late on a Sunday night, and she and her mother had driven out from Queens into the city for dinner and to see the Rockettes kick up their glittering heels.

Stranded with the dead car, Denise had gone to a pay phone and called six gas stations before reaching one in lower Manhattan that would send help.

Help arrived in the form of Angie, who manned the lumbering tow truck as if it were a sleek sports car. Perched high in the rattling tin cab, his portable cassette player broadcasting his favorite television shows (that was his hobby, taping old segments of "I Love Lucy"), he had a cigarette propped over his ear and, on the dashboard, a bag of potato chips which he munched on constantly to keep from smoking the cigarettes he was trying to give up.

He carried the cigarette in case of panic.

"Having trouble, babe?" Angie asked, jumping down from the cab and pulling on his thick gloves.

"No. I always stand in the middle of traffic in ten-degree weather with my hood in the air at midnight." She jumped up and down to keep her legs from cracking in the icy air.

"Sit in the truck. I got the heater on," he said as he helped her climb the steep steps.

He checked the engine, tried the ignition, and then yelled up to the cab, "Your starter's broken. I'll have to tow you to the garage."

Denise said, "Okay," and went across the street to the coffee shop to rescue her mother from her fifth cup of hot chocolate.

Angie drove them to catch a train home and then towed the car downtown. Two nights later Denise came back and picked up her car, and they went out for a drink.

Before her second banana daiquiri and his third beer, they discovered they had nothing in common—and laughed about it!

He was a college senior and worked in the garage part-time. She had dropped out of college after two years and worked as a secretary for an ad agency. She liked museums, classical music, and poetry. He liked horror movies, rock 'n' roll, and *Sports Illustrated*. After graduation, he was going to be a gym teacher. She didn't even know how to swim, nor did she care to learn. Summers were for tanning while reading.

"Why would anyone want to spend the rest of their life sitting at a desk?" Angie asked Denise. "Sounds boring." He scooped up the peanuts on the bar by the fistful. Smoking and drinking went together naturally—unless you could occupy your fingers throwing peanuts down your throat.

"Are you kidding? It's fun. I get to meet a lot of people. I have a lot of friends at the office, and we go to a different place every day for lunch or shopping. Besides, I make good money—probably a lot more than you make."

He laughed. She joined him. He liked that. In fact, he liked everything about her. The way she talked . . . the way she leaned forward when she was listening . . . the way her eyes smiled when the rest of her didn't.

"My mother wanted me to be a lawyer," he told her. "Nobody in my family was ever a lawyer, but like I told Mama, nobody was ever a gym teacher either." He shrugged. "In fact, up until me, nobody even finished high school."

Denise's father had been a senior clerk in the midtown main building of the post office. He had started right out of high school as a mailman in his neighborhood in Queens; over the years he had worked himself up, through steady promotions, to higher duties within the postal system. He died while Denise was still in high school.

"My father died nine years ago, leaving me, my mother, and my brother, Gaucho, who was only two years old," said Angel. "Papa was always big on education. That's all he talked about. He had tremendous respect for anyone with any kind of education. He felt about it the way some people do about religion. Anyway, after he died, Mama took the little bit of insurance money, packed us up, and brought us here for 'the good life.' " Angel grinned and downed his beer. "The good life is I'm working in a garage—and she's on welfare."

"Was it better back in Puerto Rico?" Denise asked.

"Better? It was hell! Not only wasn't there any work—there wasn't any hope. Things may be rough here, but at least it's possible for a person to amount to something."

She agreed and told him so. Before the night was over, he knew he'd have to see her again. It was easy being with her. Comfortable. She made him laugh. And aside from all that, it was nice just to sit and look at her and feel the envious stares of the other guys who passed by and noticed.

She also knew she would see him again. Eagerly. It

wasn't just that he was terrific-looking, with the biggest brown eyes and a straight, trim body and a smile that could dazzle you . . . it was that he was special. He knew it, she knew it, she knew he knew it, and there it was. He was just a special guy.

Gaucho didn't like her the first time he saw her. Angel had brought her over for dinner, and all through the meal they kept smiling at each other and laughing and giggling.

Mama didn't have a chance to say too much. She just kept passing out the food and taking away the plates from the last course. If someone had walked in, they would have thought she was the maid.

Denise tasted her first fried banana and pretended to like it a lot. Gaucho could see her working very hard to pretend. Personally, he had always hated the things and couldn't see the point of anyone pretending to like the soggy mess.

Then Denise spotted the bathtub, and that was good for five minutes of explanations and giggles.

As they left that evening, Angel hugged Mama and Gaucho. "Isn't she terrific?" he whispered.

Fortunately, he ran out of the apartment before either of them could answer.

3

Gaucho glanced down the street and a cold chill suddenly enveloped him. His heart pounded. "Oh, Jesus."

"What's wrong?" asked Mario.

Gaucho swallowed hard and mumbled, "It's him." He hid his face behind the comic book.

"What? I didn't hear you."

"Shut up, stupid," Gaucho threatened under his breath. "He's coming over here."

Mario glanced down the block. "I don't see anybody except a dumb cop."

"That's him! Shut up!"

Mario started to get worried. It wasn't like Gaucho to be afraid of anything. Certainly not a lousy cop. Unless . . .

"That cop after you?" Mario leaned over and whispered. "You do something?" Then it hit him. "You stole those comics!"

Gaucho let go and punched him in the leg. It was the only part of his body he could reach from his sitting position.

"Just be quiet and don't say anything. He's coming to the party," Gaucho warned him.

Mario was still confused.

"How do you know he's going to the party?"

Before Gaucho could answer, the cop was in front of him.

"Hey, Gaucho. How's it going?"

"Okay."

The cop gestured with his head. "Sounds like some party up there. Hope I'm not too late for the food."

Gaucho flashed his automatic smile. "I'm sure there's a lot left."

"Sure hope so." Then the cop smiled directly at Mario.

"Hi. I'm Jim Raddigan."

Mario responded nervously, "Hi."

"Well, I guess I better go up." He took off his stiff blue cap and ruffled his hair underneath. Then he put the cap back on. "Coming?"

Gaucho shook his head. "I'll be up later."

"Okay. See ya." And with that the cop bounded up the stairs, whistling.

It took a full minute for the impact to sink in. Then Mario almost exploded. "How do you know the cop? He even knew your name!"

Gaucho mumbled something.

"How come a cop is going up to your house and he's not going to arrest anybody?"

The moment Gaucho had been dreading was here. He knew he couldn't keep it a secret forever, but why did it have to come out so soon?

Gaucho stared at the ground. He couldn't look at Mario. "That cop is Angel's new brother-in-law."

Mario didn't say anything for a long while, and when he did, all he said was, "Damn." His tone was one of surprise and pity. He sat silently next to his friend, and they both stared aimlessly across the street.

For as long as he could remember, Gaucho had hated cops. No one in his family had any use for them. Cops meant only one thing—trouble. And sorrow.

Even back home in Puerto Rico police were not figures to admire. They represented power and brute force—strong men with political connections and influential friends who had little in common with the sugarcane workers or fishermen or carpenters or laborers.

If a cop came to your house, the women started crying before he could sit down.

Because he had never been in trouble, Gaucho didn't fear cops. He just hated them. He hated them for stories he had heard since he was a baby and for things he'd seen on his own.

The most contact he had with cops was whenever Mama had to go to the welfare office; she would keep Gaucho out of school so he could go with her and interpret the conversation with the social worker.

As they sat in the long line of benches in the huge, dingy waiting room, Gaucho's attention would be drawn to the two cops on duty. Now and then one would yell out, "Keep that kid quiet!" But mostly they would just stand and talk to each other and laugh. The only people who laughed in the welfare office were cops and social workers.

Mama's attitude was, "Somebody has to do the job. You treat them nice, they treat you nice."

Maybe at one time Gaucho could've accepted this philosophy. But not now. Not after Benny.

Benny was the neighborhood character. He could make you laugh just in anticipation. He was a natural clown and was always doing something crazy. Whatever the latest fad was, Benny would be the first one to try it out.

If you were sitting on the stoop and saw him coming your way, you'd start smiling automatically—before he even got close. Then when he got to you, he'd say something wacky or do some imitation of a television commercial. He never came up dry.

Since his folks were the supers of the building across the street, Benny had a spare room in the basement which he turned into a clubhouse, complete with weights, games, a pool table, and a basketball hoop. He even had a jukebox and a refrigerator.

Even though Benny was four years older, he never made Gaucho feel like a jerky little kid. In fact, Gaucho was welcome anytime in the clubhouse, even when the older guys were there drinking beer and smoking pot.

On those occasions, Gaucho would occupy himself at the jukebox or the pool table. He was afraid to try any kind of drugs, and the first time he smoked a cigarette he got dizzy and his stomach hurt. He had never tasted such a lousy thing in his life. He couldn't understand what all the fun was.

Benny and his friends never tried to convert Gaucho. If he wanted something—it was there. If not—that was okay, too.

The only time Gaucho would be excluded was when Benny showed dirty movies.

"I'd let you stay, only we gonna have a little party with some girls after and . . . you know . . ."

Gaucho knew. He and Mario had seen enough dirty pictures in magazines and heard enough stories around school. To tell the truth, it all sounded vaguely disgusting. And boring.

But maybe there was something to it, if Benny liked it.

Benny was his hero. There was no problem too small, too large, too embarrassing, too silly, too scary, that

Gaucho couldn't discuss with his friend. If Benny didn't have a solution, he would come right out and say, "Hey, man. I don't know what to tell ya."

Then they'd both laugh and the problem wouldn't seem so terrible.

Another thing Gaucho liked about Benny was that if you noticed—really looked at him objectively—you would realize that Benny was probably the homeliest kid ever born. He was tall and skinny and had ears that stuck out even under his hair, and his face was pocked from pimples. And even with all that and his teeth, which were crooked and rotting—there wasn't anyone more popular.

Gaucho never noticed Benny was homely. Anybody that Gaucho liked a lot was beautiful to him. He only noticed after Mama pointed it out, saying, "You see, *hijo*. You don't have to be pretty to be happy." Gaucho was glad to hear that. He wasn't too crazy about his own looks.

"You'll be okay. It's just that your body and your face ain't come together yet. Couple of years, it'll all work out," Benny had consoled him. "Look, man, anybody with a brother like you got and an ol' lady who still looks terrific ain't got nothing to worry about."

Benny could always make him feel better.

Then one night, two summers ago, about midnight, two police cars screeched into the neighborhood. The cops bolted from the cars, ran into the building, and raced to the roof. A report had come to the precinct that there was a burglary in progress.

Groping through the darkness, one of the cops heard the creaking of the roof door behind him. Instantly he spun around and fired.

Benny lay dead. Beside him was a laundry basket filled with wet clothes. He had gone to hang out the wash for his mother.

It didn't take long for the news to spread to the whole neighborhood.

Awakened out of a deep sleep by the ambulance siren, Gaucho sat numbly on the fire escape, looking down across the street. The flashing red lights of the police cars bounced off the brick walls and invaded the silent, dark, brooding apartments. People stood like motionless silhouettes, quietly watching the drama unfold. The yellow beacon from the ambulance chased the red spots in the air.

Hundreds watched, but no one uttered a word. The only sound was the crackling static of the police radios.

Then came the worst sound of all. The screams from Benny's mother.

Gaucho watched the white-uniformed men hurrying with the stretcher. Their white shoes were silent on the cement steps.

Then Benny's mother screamed again.

Two weeks later the cop who shot Benny was suspended from the force, and it was learned that the cops had been at the wrong address.

There had been other incidents before Benny and since.

Once Gaucho was walking home from school and was halted by a cop who made him stand still for a search. Gaucho started to ask what was wrong but was warned, "Shut up, spic!"

Another time, down in the park during a softball game, Angel got in an argument with a cop who made some casual remark as he strolled by. Angel exploded and raced after him. Angel went home with a bloody face and a new space between his front teeth.

For Gaucho, who witnessed the fight and was too frightened to help, it was easy to hate cops.

4

"You mean you got a *cop* in your family!" Mario finally spat out the words.

"Yeah."

Mario shook his head gravely. "Damn."

Gaucho avoided his eyes.

After another long silence, Mario got up the courage to ask, "What are you gonna do when the guys find out?"

Gaucho now turned and looked straight at him. "I'm hoping the guys don't find out. Ever. Understand?"

Mario nodded. "Yeah." Then he paced around a bit, now and then glancing up at the window. "Look, man. I'll see you later." Mario jumped from the stoop and walked down the block toward the park.

Gaucho watched him till he was out of view and wondered if he had lost his oldest friend. He wished he were lying in his bed with the curtain drawn and his face under the pillow.

"Hey! *Que pasa, hombre!*"

Gaucho leaped in midair and spun to embrace his uncle.

"Stop. It's too hot." Pachecko laughed, easing him down. "I had to get away," he said, wiping his brow with a handkerchief the size of a towel. "Those crazy women up there won't leave me alone. All they want to do is dance and put their arms around me and kiss me and tell me how pretty I am. Swear to God, I had to sneak out the door. And then I come here and you start kissing me!"

Gaucho laughed.

Pachecko leaned over and planted a wet, loud kiss on Gaucho's cheek. "There! And that's all you get, 'cause I gotta save it for my girlfriend in the Bronx."

Gaucho smiled. Just looking at his uncle made him happy.

Pachecko was a carnival to behold. Today he wore a yellow jacket with brown squares, a wide maroon tie with beige stripes, brown slacks, a yellow shirt, and black and white saddle shoes with white socks. Jutting out from his jacket pocket was a bright pink handkerchief that matched the huge pink stone in his gold ring. The ring matched his front teeth, which glistened with gold. All of this was topped off by a wide straw hat with a lettuce-green band.

"How come you not happy?" Pachecko asked, lowering his wide, flabby body to the steps.

"What do you mean, *Tio?*"

"Don't tell me, what do you mean? I saw you before sitting here like that. Same thing at the church. I was watching."

Gaucho shrugged.

"You and me, I thought we always told each other everything. Didn't I tell you since you were a baby, 'Gaucho, you got a problem, anything wrong, you come to me.' So. . . ." He waited.

Gaucho hesitated and then blurted, "Where's your car?"

Pachecko pointed up the block. "Same place I always keep it." He meant the fire hydrant near the corner. He always parked at fire hydrants so that his car would be protected from dents by other drivers trying to park their cars.

This year Pachecko was driving a green and white Cadillac with leopard-skin seat covers and green carpeting two inches thick. Before riding with him, you had to take off your shoes. And not even the President of the United States, Pachecko was fond of repeating, could eat an ice cream cone on the front seat. No one was allowed to sit on the back seat, which was crammed with furry white throw pillows surrounding a stuffed yellow panda.

"You gonna tell me what's wrong, or you gonna make me sit here all afternoon under this miserable sun and guess?"

"It's nothing," Gaucho said brightly.

Pachecko reached into his jacket pocket and produced

a can of beer. He pried the top up with his long pinky nail. "Want some?"

Gaucho took a long, thirsty swallow.

"Okay. I didn't say drink the whole thing." Pachecko wiped the aluminum top with his handkerchief and rolled the icy can back and forth over his forehead.

"I'm gonna take a wild guess that you're not too happy that your brother got married with that girl."

Gaucho didn't respond.

"So what if you don't like her? You don't have to like her. Just 'cause she married your brother don't mean you have to like her. On Christmas you send her a card— and that's it."

Gaucho sighed. Why was Pachecko making him think about it? Why didn't he tell him one of his many stories instead? Why was everyone after him all day? Was it so terrible just to want to be alone and not talk?

"Tell you the truth, *hombre*, I'm not too crazy about her either. Not that she's not friendly. She tries. Maybe too hard. I don't know. But something about her reminds me of Señora Barracuda."

Gaucho glanced up at his uncle with a mischievous glint in his eye. Was he leading into one of his stories?

Pachecko pretended not to notice Gaucho's sudden interest in him and casually reached into his other pocket and pulled out a cigar. He took his time tearing open the cellophane wrapping and removing the gold paper ring, which he automatically handed to Gaucho; then he wet the end with his tongue and snipped off the front. Then, slowly, he reached in his pants pocket for the gold lighter and flicked on the flame. He brought the flame to the cigar and puffed, loudly sucking in air. He repeated this a few times.

Gaucho finally screamed, "Tell me!"

Pachecko turned to him innocently. "Tell you what, *hombre?*" He held the cigar in midair.

"About Señora Barracuda!" Gaucho pounded his fists against his legs.

"Oh," Pachecko said, exhaling a balloon of smoke. Then he looked at Gaucho and winked. "You force me."

Gaucho stretched out comfortably and leaned his weight on his elbow.

Pachecko rested his back against the iron railing of the stoop and flicked his ashes in the nearby garbage can.

"It's a true story, what I'm gonna tell you. Happened a long time ago, when I was a little boy. I was just a baby. My mama told me the story. Anyway, we had this mayor back home who loved to fish. That's all the man lived for. In the morning he would jump out of bed, run down to the ocean, and scream, 'Hey, fish! Stay there. I be back.'

"Then he would go to city hall and do his work, and when he finish he run back to the water and jump in the boat with his friends and spend the whole night fishing. One night a big storm came up and the mayor and everybody on the boat drowned. The storm turned the boat upside down, and a week later they found pieces of the boat on the beach.

"So now the mayor's wife becomes mayor and the first thing she did in city hall was make a new law: 'No fishing.' And that law meant just what she said. No fishing. Anybody who fished went to jail."

Gaucho sat up straight. "Damn. What was she, crazy?"

"Sure. All those years of being alone in the house with her husband out fishing drove her crazy. At first nobody paid attention to the law and they went fishing like always, but then when they got back the police were there on the sand waiting, and all the fishermen went right to jail.

"Pretty soon all the men of the village were in jail and families were starving. You see, *hijo,* the men didn't go fishing just because it was fun—they went to feed their families. For poor people, the ocean is like a supermarket that is run for free.

"So now . . . the fish start to get bigger. Sure. With nobody to chase them they just float around and eat and get fat like whales.

"One day, my cousin Armando, he was about your age, he's walking on the beach hoping to find some crabs to bring home, when all of a sudden he sees this big fat ugly monster of a fish with jelly eyes lying on the sand."

"What did Armando do?" asked Gaucho.

"He got sick. The thing was so ugly he got sick.

Thank God it was dead. A thing that ugly—alive—could make a lot of trouble. So then Armando got the idea. It came to him just like that. Now, you have to remember that his father and his brother and his three cousins are in jail—for fishing!"

Gaucho squirmed. "What did he do?"

"The first thing he did was to bury it. He covered it with palmetto leaves and palms and threw sand all over them to keep the mosquitoes away. Then he ran into the village and got all the young people together and all the old men and some of the women and took them to where the fish was.

"They dug the fish out and hid it behind the mango trees until it got dark. Very dark. They even waited for the moon to go behind the clouds. Then when it was dark and quiet, the army of children and old men and women started dragging the monster into town. They tied a rope around the fish's belly and dragged it—being very quiet—right to the porch of the mayor's house.

"Armando and some of his friends climbed on the roof—very quiet—and pulled the ugly fish up by the rope. Then they tied the rope to a tree and let the fish hang down in front of the door—with the jelly eyes open and the pink and red gums hanging open."

Pachecko shivered. "Make me sick just to think of it."

"Then, Armando and his friends hide under the porch and all together—but very soft—they start calling—very low, like voices from a grave . . . 'Señora . . . Señora

. . . Señora . . .' Just then a cold wind started to blow, and the trees started to bend. Even the moon was afraid to come out. The sky was black. . . .

" 'Señora . . . Señora . . .' the voices called from the grave. 'Señora . . .'

"Inside the house, the mayor's wife wakes up, turns on the light, and gets out of bed. She walks to the front door, opens it—and just that moment the moon jumped out and shone the light on the ugly monster!

"The woman screamed and started running. She ran yelling into town, through town, and out of town.

"Nobody ever saw her again."

"And what happened to all the people in jail?" Gaucho asked.

"They got let go. Today, in that village, on the beach they have a statue of the fish. The statue is so ugly none of the birds will sit on it. *But*—it reminds the people that no matter how bad things are, they can be worse."

Gaucho grinned. "That didn't really happen."

Pachecko shrugged. "If you say so." He leaned back and stretched out his legs, pulling up his white socks. He stole a glance at his nephew. At least now Gaucho was smiling.

"Did I ever tell you how you got your name?" Pachecko asked.

"No." Gaucho's face lit up. "Tell me."

"Boy, that was some day." He puffed on his cigar. "I'm sure I must have told you."

"No. Never. I swear."

Pachecko studied him closely. "You sure?"

"Positive."

"Okay." Pachecko slapped him on the leg. If there was one thing in life he enjoyed more than drinking cold beer on a hot Sunday, it was telling a story. He sat up straight.

"You were born in your grandmother's bed. You know that?"

Gaucho smiled. "Mama told me."

"I'll never forget that day. It was so hot the sweat would roll into your face and eyes like rain. Me and my brother, your papa, were working in your grandmother's back yard. The pigs had knocked down the fence again and the chickens were running around. I remember your mother was sitting on the porch sewing, and then the next thing we know everybody is in the house—all excited, people yelling—and then before you know it there you are! Just like that. Even the chickens got in the house 'cause nobody remembered to close the door. I tell you, it was like a circus. People laughing, crying, yelling, your poor grandfather almost fainted—and in the middle of all this, there you are, in the middle of the big bed, crying and waving your hands. So that's how you got your name!"

Gaucho thought about it for a long moment. "But how?"

"Well, when your father saw you with the feet kicking and the hands making circles in the air, it reminded him of a gaucho with his rope doing tricks. A gaucho is a cowboy in South America. So—you became Gaucho." Pachecko reached over and stroked the boy's hair. "How come nobody told you the story?"

Gaucho lowered his head. "You know Mama never mentions Papa. She gets too sad. Even when she looks at his picture she gets sad."

Pachecko reached over and hugged him close.

"Just because your papa is upstairs with God drinking rum and playing dominoes doesn't mean we can't talk about him. He was my brother and I still love him very much. I think about him like he was back home. That way I don't miss him so much."

Gaucho could feel tears trying to break through. He tightened his body against them.

"Why did we have to come here, anyway? I hate it here!"

Pachecko released his hold. "Hey. Take it easy, *hombre.*"

"It's true. I hate it! I wanna go home. There's nothing here for me. You tell me all those stories about fishing and riding bikes over the bridge to go to town and staying out all night with your friends—I never did anything like that. I can't. I can't even go to the candy store alone. You talk about pigs and chickens—I can't even have a dog. And even if Mama could buy me a bicycle, somebody would steal it. Mario had two stolen in the park. So you tell me, *Tio*. What are we doing here?" The tears came silently.

"You here because you have better opportunity. Your mama brought you and Angel so you could go to good schools and become someone important. Do you realize that your brother is the first one in the whole family ever to go to college? Back home, young men can't go to college. Oh, they have the college, but the young men are needed to work and help support the family. Who has money to feed the family back home while the young go to school? Can't be done. Here it is possible."

"So what! He goes to college and at night he fixes cars. Big deal. I'd rather cut sugarcane."

Pachecko laughed, a bitter laugh. "You say that. You don't know what it's like to be in that sun every day of your life, crawling, sweating, cutting, getting bit by mosquitoes, looking out for snakes! And for what? A few pennies an hour. No. Your mama did the right thing. Here you get an education and then you get a good job, a clean job inside an office, and you save your money and go home whenever you want for a vacation. That's what I do."

Gaucho swiped at the tears with his shoulder. "For years Angel has been promising that when he graduates from college we would all go back home. He said we were going to get a house and I could have two dogs and Mama could have a garden to grow flowers. He promised. And I believed him. He lied to me!"

Pachecko tried to be cheerful. "Hey, maybe he still plans to go. So he takes his wife along. So what? What do you care as long as you go."

Gaucho shook his head slowly. "No, *Tio*. This morning when we rode to the church, I asked him when we're going home. He told me, 'This is my home now.' "

Gaucho's voice quivered. "We're never going home."

5

"Smile," someone shouted as flashbulbs popped around the couple cutting the four-tiered whipped-cream wedding cake.

"Come on, man, kiss 'er," another voice called out. Angel did so, to much laughter and applause.

From where he was propped against the radiator pipes in the living room, Jim Raddigan pleasantly declined a beer. "Technically, I'm on duty. I have to report to the precinct soon."

Angel slapped him on the back. "Hey, brother, you know what the merengue is?"

"Sure." Jim smiled. "It's that white stuff you pile up on lemon pie."

Those who were nearby howled! Those who hadn't overheard were soon broadcast the story, and still others waited for the Spanish translation—and then they all howled.

"Jerk. It's a dance, man. Like this."

The music blaring, Angel swooped his mother into his arms and propelled her across the floor, swaying with a rhythmic bounce as the guests formed a circle around them and clapped their hands to the beat.

"Arriba! Arriba!" they chanted.

Mama tossed back her long black hair and lifted the hem of her dress over her knees. With her other hand on her hip, she shook her body till every inch rippled.

"Tell it to me! Tell it to me!" Mario's father beat out the rhythm by hitting two beer cans together. "You got it!"

Angel surrendered to the music, proudly parading Mama across the room. He whipped off his tie and tuxedo jacket and rolled up his sleeves, never missing a beat.

He stole a glance at Denise, who had a strange smile on her face.

Jim noticed also and approached his sister. "That's some dance, huh?"

Denise nodded gamely. "Yeah."

She would have liked to sit down for a few minutes, in a corner alone somewhere, but the apartment was so small there wasn't a corner that wasn't crowded.

She had never seen so many people with so much energy. Wasn't there any such thing as slow Spanish music?

"It's a hell of a party," Jim commented. "Having fun?"

"I would if I understood the language," she said,

smiling widely at a couple who toasted her from across the room. "Another hour of this and my skin will crack. I've smiled more today than I have in my whole life."

"Well, just keep it up a little longer and no one will guess you're having a terrible time," Jim said with a hint of sarcasm.

"Look. It's just that I'm tired and that damn music hasn't stopped for a minute. Good thing Mother didn't come. The heat alone would have killed her. There's not even a fan in the window. How do they stand it?"

Jim filled some champagne glasses and handed them out. If he was making a determined effort to be friendly and outgoing, it might be because inside he was very angry at his mother for suddenly developing a "head-ache" and not coming to the reception.

After the wedding, there had been a smaller reception in the church rectory for the Raddigans' friends and relatives and Denise's co-workers. Her mother had felt that it was asking too much to have all those people travel from Queens to Manhattan, so it had been decided to hold two receptions—but the plan called for Mother to attend both and meet Angel's friends and relatives. However, shortly before they left the church, Mother had developed a headache. It came as no surprise to Jim.

Denise stood near the open window and tried to wave some of the fresh air onto the back of her neck.

Just then Angel approached her, led her to the center of the room, and followed the commands of the photographer, who posed Denise with her long silk train spread out in front of her. More pictures were taken of her opening the many gifts piled on the table in the kitchen. This was followed by a formal family picture of Angel and Denise and Mama and Jim, taken in the living room.

"Wait! Wait for Gaucho," Mama said anxiously.

"Hell with him," Angel said, smiling for the camera.

6

That night, long after the party, Gaucho lay in his tiny room—if he stretched out both arms he could touch the walls from his bed—and tried to figure out a way to make enough money to get himself and Mama back home.

It seemed rather hopeless. The only person he knew who had any money was Uncle Pachecko, and Mama would never accept any help from him. Although Mama did love him, as one is obligated to love another member of the family, she nonetheless strictly disapproved of his life-style and the way he earned his money. He was a bookmaker and a numbers man.

Spanish people all over the city played daily numbers with Pachecko. His American clients placed their sports bets with him. He had a thriving business because in a short time he had earned a reputation for honesty. If a person's number came up, they would be paid that same day. Few bookies in the city enjoyed as large and loyal a following. So loyal were his clients that on the many occasions when Pachecko was arrested and thrown in jail, no one placed their action with any of the competition, preferring to wait till Pachecko was freed.

His large business volume afforded him the new Cadillacs every year, the annual trip home, and a nice apartment in the Bronx. Whatever money was left over went to bribing judges and cops and to lawyers' fees. "I have expenses just like any other businessman," Pachecko once told his nephew.

No. Gaucho would have to get the money on his own. Somehow. He concentrated on finding a way.

In his neighborhood, there were various ways to earn money. Like Papo, for instance. Everyone knew that he sold drugs. His family was the only one on the block with two color televisions and real rugs on the floor. Not the cold linoleum with the flower patterns that everyone else had. Papo's apartment was also the only one with bars and a gate across the window. He lived in the constant fear that junkies would try to break in, thinking he kept his stuff there. That's why Papo also had a German shepherd dog, and a gun that he kept concealed in the shoe bag hanging on the inside of his closet door.

As far as his parents knew, Papo, the high school dropout, worked as a busboy in a downtown Spanish restaurant and made good tips.

Then there was tall, funky, Afro-haired Leon, who had various enterprises, including a part-time job he performed one night a week for which he was paid as much as two hundred dollars. The job itself was easy. All he had to do was sit on his living room couch, look out the window at the street below, and in the event of anything suspicious—like two strangers milling about . . . a car that kept circling the block—he would pick up his phone, dial the number across the hall, and alert the poker players of possible danger.

For this boring job, which could consume as much as ten to sixteen hours, Leon was well paid. And from his pay, he would reimburse a trusted assistant who would keep the watch while Leon went to the bathroom or fixed a snack.

Maybe Gaucho could be Leon's assistant. He could tell his mother he was spending the night, and since Leon lived in the next building, she wouldn't have anything to worry about. Macho, who was Leon's closest buddy and his usual assistant, had recently gone to jail for robbery, so maybe there was a chance. He would look for Leon first thing in the morning. He wondered what Leon paid his assistants.

"*Hijo.*" Mama gently slid the curtain aside. "Are you awake?"

Gaucho hesitated. He didn't feel like talking. Especially after all that had happened that day.

"Gauchito," she said softly. It was a voice that didn't want to wake him, but if it accidentally did—she wouldn't be too unhappy.

He sighed. "Yes, Mamacita. I'm awake."

Mama entered the room quietly, her silhouette framed in the orange candle glow from the kitchen.

Every night after the dishes were done and the floor swept and the garbage taken down, Mama would turn off the kitchen light like a shopkeeper closing her store after a long day.

Then she would light the candle that stood on the counter next to the refrigerator. Behind the candle stood the porcelain statues of Joseph and the Virgin Mary. In front of the statues she placed each night a fresh dish of water. Tonight the accompanying vases held real flowers, in honor of Angel's wedding.

The warm smell of candle wax burning filtered through to Gaucho's room.

"Tired, *hijo?*" Mama asked, sitting on the edge of the cot.

"Yes." He yawned. He turned on his side so Mama would have more room to sit.

Mama reached down and stroked his thick hair. Whenever he was within range, Mama would touch his face, fix his clothes, brush back his hair, squeeze his arm. . . . She used to do it all the time in front of his friends till he asked her to stop. He noticed now she only touched him when they were alone—and barely even then. He wondered suddenly if he had hurt her feelings back then.

"You look tired," she said. He could tell by the sound of her voice that she was smiling.

"How can you tell? It's too dark."

Mama pinched his ear. "I can tell."

He decided he wasn't that sleepy after all. "Mama. Any cake left?"

"Aha! Now you're hungry! All day I tried to get you to come up. All day you sit downstairs and don't listen to me, and now that it's almost ten o'clock and you have to get up early tomorrow for school—now you're hungry!"

"All right. Forget it."

Mama leaned over and kissed him. *"Vamos."*

He sprang out of bed and followed her to the kitchen, where she took out a large, thick slice of cake from the bread box. "I have two more big pieces which Señora Cabrera is saving for me in her freezer. That way you can have cake for breakfast all week if you want. And I also saved you this," Mama said, emptying the refrigerator of cookies, watermelon, sandwiches, meat turnovers, and rice and beans.

"Just tell me what you want and I heat it up," she said, setting a napkin and fork by his plate.

Gaucho opted for a little bit of everything and happily sat down to eat.

"Can you imagine that right now your brother and Denise are somewhere in Miami Beach! And just not too long ago they were here sitting in this kitchen." Her voice registered a slight nervousness.

"I told him to call from the airport as soon as he got there. I told him to call Señora Cabrera and she would bang on the ceiling and let me know. . . ." She glanced upward.

Something was wrong and Gaucho couldn't quite figure it out. Something was different. He stopped eating and looked around. Something . . .

The television! Of course! He and Mama were in the kitchen and the television was on—loudly. His mother never allowed the television to be on if no one was in the living room watching it. That was her strictest rule, because it involved wasting electricity and therefore money.

Another thing—she never turned the volume up. She couldn't tolerate the noise. Whenever Gaucho watched his programs, he practically had to read the actors' lips.

Then it came to him! She had purposely left the television on to hear of any plane crashes. Had to be. He tested her. "Mama. You forgot to turn off the TV."

She wiped the stove. "Just eat."

The doorbell rang. It was Señora Rivera and her two sons and her daughter from the first floor, loaded down with electric appliances, a television, a stereo, and a thick gold living room rug.

"*Muchas gracias,* Maria," she told Gaucho's mother as she directed her army where to place the objects. They stacked them neatly in a corner of the living room. "We come back tomorrow night." She waved as they departed.

It was such a normal ritual that no discussion was

necessary. Tomorrow was the first of the month. Therefore the Rivera's social worker from the welfare department might stop by to pay a surprise visit, and it wouldn't do to have her find all these items which the City of New York considered luxuries.

The welfare check was to cover rent, food, utilities, and some clothes. It was carefully calculated to avoid any "extra" items. If a family on welfare suddenly acquired a television or stereo or new linoleum or a dish cabinet, the financial source had to be disclosed. If it was a gift from a relative, then that relative would be contacted and told if they could be that generous, they could support the family. One mother in the neighborhood was bounced off welfare for owning a microwave oven. Her son had stolen it from an appliance store during a riot, but the woman told the social worker that her boyfriend had given it to her. "Good," said the social worker. "He can also buy you the food that goes in it."

Gaucho's mother was allowed to have her television because it was an old, used, cheap model that she bought for twenty-five dollars from the shoemaker.

One Christmas, Pachecko gave Mama and Gaucho a large, shiny mahogany television console with an AM/FM radio and stereo tape deck complete with headset and an automatic turntable. Mama finally sold it because it was too heavy for her and Gaucho to lug upstairs once a month.

7

"No way, man!" Leon had told him as he sucked the last of the Italian ice from the soggy paper cup. "I already got a guy. Besides, the work can be dangerous." He smiled. "Come back and talk to me in about five years."

Gaucho shot him a look of disgust. "I ain't no baby, you know. I know what's happening and I won't need your lousy job in five years!"

"Hey, come on, I didn't mean nothing wrong. I just ain't got no work right now. But—if something comes up, I hear of anything—I'll let you know. Okay?"

Gaucho had tossed the basketball at him and left the playground. That was one of three people he had approached for work who had turned him down. The next one he'd asked was ol' man Pinky.

"What can you do? I got a broom bigger than you!"

Gaucho said he could sweep the sidewalk, stack the newspapers, straighten the magazine rack.

"If you and your friends didn't steal me blind, I might be able to afford to hire some help."

Gaucho paid for his chocolate soda and left. He went directly to Armando's Bodega y Carniceria. This was where Mama bought all her groceries on credit and paid for them at the end of the month.

Every day after school, Gaucho would go to the store with Mama's list, written in Spanish, and Armando would get the various items from the shelves or the meat case in the back of the store. Then he would total up the bill and write the amount in a large, heavy notebook he kept behind the counter. He would also write the same amount in the little pocket notebook that Gaucho presented to him. That way Armando and Mama kept the same records. Mama's notebook was old and grease-stained, and the pencil markings of past months were hardly legible. When she received her monthly check and paid her bill, Armando would run a red line through the numbers to show she was caught up. The book was filled with smudged red lines.

One time, a few years earlier, Gaucho had gone to the store with a new friend, Tommy Murphy, who had just moved into the neighborhood and was assigned to Gaucho's class. Gaucho had been invited to Tommy's house after school, and they had played in his large room with his train set. Then, just before dinner, Tommy's mother asked him to go to the store for a head of lettuce. Gaucho walked with him, and as they stood by the vegetable counter, he blurted out, "You forgot to get the book!"

Tommy didn't know what his new friend was talking about. Gaucho kept explaining about the book—otherwise they wouldn't give him the head of lettuce.

Tommy shrugged, took out a dollar, and paid the woman. She gave him some change and the lettuce.

That was the most amazing thing Gaucho had ever seen.

"Sorry, Gaucho," Armando said as he crouched in front of his store, wiping the dirty water from the plate-glass window. "I'd like to help you, but my sister and her kids just moved in with me, and they help me with deliveries and cleaning and whatever I need them to do." He dunked the sponge stick in the sudsy water. "But if they ever leave, I'll let you know. Right now, I'm sorry."

Gaucho told him he understood and started walking home. He spotted Mario's chunky form ahead of him and ran to catch up.

"Hi," he said, falling into step alongside Mario.

"Hi," Mario slurped, biting into a slice of pizza.

"What do you do when you need money?" Gaucho asked.

"Easy. I take it out of my mother's purse when she's not looking."

"I mean a lot of money. Not nickels and dimes. More like fifty—a hundred dollars."

Mario choked.

Gaucho hit him in the back. "You okay?"

"Yeah. Yeah. It was the hot pepper."

They reached their stoop and sat down.

"What do you need all that money for?"

"I just do, that's all."

"Nobody in the world has that much money except maybe your uncle Pachecko. You ask him for it?"

Gaucho shook his head. "I don't want to unless I have to. There has to be somewhere I can get it."

"Gaucho." He heard his mother's voice behind him. "Come, *hijo,* we have to go to *la marqueta.*"

"Right now?"

"*Sí.* Your brother called from Miami. He and Denise are coming back tonight and they gonna have dinner with us, so we have to hurry. Come on."

"Why do I have to go? I got things to do," he wailed.

"Because I have too much to carry. Don't worry. I'm gonna give you fifty cents."

"Let's go," he said, and they headed for the subway.

Mama had been very pleased with herself the first time she picked up her shopping bag and went marketing alone. Her first few years in New York, she wouldn't even go to the neighborhood stores by herself for fear she'd get lost and not be able to find her way home. Since she couldn't read any English—and therefore couldn't understand signs—and since her spoken English was so poor, the possibilities were very real and frightening. She could get lost and never find her apartment again.

So everywhere she went, she depended on her dear

friend, Señora Cabrera, to get her there and back. One day Mario's mother had an earache and couldn't go shopping, so rather than disappoint Gaucho, who had asked for chicken and rice, Mama decided, timidly, to brave the trip alone.

It was the beginning of Mama's gaining confidence. She started to believe that she could survive in this strange country.

Soon she grew bolder and explored new neighborhoods, new shops, new sections of the city. Once she and Gaucho, more through instinct than knowledge, rode on a long series of buses and subways and made it all the way out to Coney Island, where they spent a great day on the beach. In the evening they walked the colorful boardwalk, ate hot corn on the cob and greasy french fries with vinegar, and even went on a few of the tamer rides. She was still proud of the fact that they got home that night without asking anyone for directions.

As Mama's confidence grew, so did her desire to build a better life. At each store where the proprietor spoke Spanish, Mama would inquire if there was any work available. With Angel in high school and Gaucho in first grade at the time, and no income except what was left from her husband's insurance policy, things were starting to become desperate.

In one store, the man barked at her, "How can you work, woman! You don't even speak English. How do you expect to talk with the customers? Sign language?"

A few people overheard the outburst, and Mama felt

tears rush to her eyes in embarrassment. She fled the store and walked home quickly, more determined than ever that her children would never suffer such humiliation.

With Angel due to graduate soon from high school, Mama knew she had to do something quickly if he was to go to college.

The very next day, with her friend Señora Cabrera, Mama went downtown to the welfare office and pleaded for help for herself and her children.

It took the entire summer for her case to be processed and investigated, but she was finally approved. Three things worked in her favor. One, she was medically unable to work full-time because she had chronic asthma; two, she was a widow with two sons to support; and three, she had no relatives living in the country.

Mama didn't want to lie about Pachecko, but she could not mention him for fear they would find out how he earned his living and send him to jail.

Mama found lying difficult and unpleasant. It was a trait she disliked in others and would not tolerate in her children or anyone she loved. Her resentment of Pachecko grew because he was responsible for her having to lie.

Along with the lies went the daily fear that she would be found out and thrown into jail. Every day in the Spanish newspaper *El Diario* there were stories of welfare cheaters being sentenced to jail.

Still . . . it was all worth it if her sons could go to college.

Gaucho swayed from side to side with the motion of the subway car. He stood reading the colorful map on the wall which traced all the various stops and routes. Somehow, one of those thin marks would get him to the Bronx. He hoped he wouldn't have to make that trip and involve Pachecko.

If he could raise the money himself to get him and Mama back home, it would mean that he had succeeded where his big college-graduate brother had failed. The family, everyone, would know who the real "man" was.

Mama and Gaucho got off the train at Lexington Avenue and 116th Street. Once on the sidewalk, they were immediately engulfed by *la marqueta*.

La marqueta was an area of approximately fifteen blocks made up of sidewalk stands and stores offering all types of merchandise for sale. The items were displayed on the sidewalk right on the pavement or on tables or the hoods of cars. Many of the clothes were hung on hangers and fastened to clotheslines that dangled above the shoppers' heads. The store owners competed for the customers' attention by calling out to them as they strolled by.

"*Entra! Entra!* Plenty more inside. Just today—everything ten percent off."

On every street corner stood the food vendors with their unique wares. Some sold little balls of coconut candy covered with chocolate, vanilla, and strawberry. Others sold meat pies in thin triangle-shaped crusts filled with juicy hamburger meat and onions. Gaucho's favorite was the paper cups filled with shaved ice, swimming in root beer syrup. Mama preferred the cherry flavor. Gaucho liked to watch the man slide the steel shaver across the large hunk of ice and dunk the tiny slivers of snow into the paper cup. If you smiled a lot, the guy would always give you an extra dash of syrup from the large round bottle with the skinny neck.

There also were blocks of indoor stands, sheltered in a huge, wide tunnel underneath the elevated railroad tracks. Inside this area, which resembled an airplane hangar, you could buy silver sequins by the yard, floral slipcovers, shower curtains, carpeting, loose-leaf paper, paint, live chickens, shoes, dinner plates, chalk, or even a color television set.

Here the vendors also shouted out their wares in Spanish and English, holding up various items. One man drew much attention with a live chicken that sat on his shoulder, somewhat bored, as the man waited on customers and added up their purchases.

Gaucho never tired of it. To him, *la marqueta* was one huge carnival. Especially on the rare days when he had money to spend, and today he still had a little left from the money Pachecko had given him.

Mama headed for the vegetable stand to buy the fat green bananas she would cut up and fry in hot lard, and the green-black avocado that she would squeeze firmly as she asked the man, "You sure this one is good enough for tonight?" The man would throw it in the air, catch it in his thick fingers, and say, "Perfect." And he was always right.

Gaucho maneuvered Mama near the stand with all the threads, buttons, and lace. The man who ran that stand also sold the freshest and tastiest candy. Huge glass jars lined his table, filled with one sugary delight after the other.

Mama reached into her shopping bag and pulled out her big purse. Then she dug into her purse and came out with her small brown leather change purse. She took out two quarters.

"Get what you want and meet me by the fish."

Alone with his money and all the candy spread in front of him, it took Gaucho almost ten minutes to decide. He finally chose five pieces of everything the man had in stock. It cost him the whole fifty cents and most of his other money, but he didn't care. The candy filled up a chunky paper bag, and he liked looking inside to see all the different colors and flavors crowded together.

He made his way to the fish counter and spotted Mama leaning against the glass case, pointing out her selection to the man in the white apron.

"How many, lady?"

"*Una dozena.*"

Gaucho groaned. The thing he most dreaded was happening before him. His anger started to churn as he watched his mother smiling and casually pointing to the blue-shell crabs inside the glass case. The crabs were lumped on top of each other like a living mountain. Claws and legs stretched out as the creatures climbed over the other slick, slippery bodies, reaching the top of the crab pyramid only to cascade to the bottom again.

The aproned man reached into the case, picked out a dozen by their claws, and dropped them into a paper bag.

Mama handed the bag to Gaucho without looking at him. She knew. And what really got him annoyed was that he knew that she knew. They walked silently to the subway. Now and then Gaucho would mumble some irritation.

Mama felt guilty. She'd make it up to him, she told herself. She loved to eat crabs, she loved to cook crabs, but she hated to carry them. And someone had to.

Gaucho stood on the platform, cursing the subway that didn't arrive. The twelve captive crabs clawed and attacked the paper bag from within. Gaucho held the brown bag in a death grip between two taut fingers.

"If we took a cab, we'd be home already," he growled.

"And what would you eat for lunch all week? Bread and mustard? Cabs cost money, you know."

The train finally thundered into the station, and he and Mama took two empty seats near the door. He was certain everyone was looking at him. Surely everyone could hear the crabs fighting to get out. Gaucho carefully placed the bag on the seat between him and Mama, hoping their bodies would conceal some of the noise.

Once, about a year ago, Gaucho was holding a similar bag out in front of him when a person getting off the train hurried past, knocking the bag on the floor—and six crabs hastily escaped.

So did everyone else in the car. People ran out screaming. The conductor and two Transit Authority policemen dashed into the car and found Gaucho and his mother on their knees, scurrying after a gang of crabs. Using Gaucho's sneakers and the conductor's cap, they finally trapped the crabs, delaying the subway train for twenty minutes.

Fortunately, the conductor was also Puerto Rican and enjoyed a crab dish now and then. Still, it had been one of the most humiliating experiences of Gaucho's life, and he still broke out in a cold sweat whenever he thought of it.

He glanced casually at the brown paper bag—not wanting to draw attention to it—and saw the first of what he knew would be many, many tiny holes that would appear before he got home.

A thin sliver of blue claw poked through the bag, and Gaucho shot his mother a dirty look.

"If they get out, I'm getting up and leaving like I don't know nothing," he whispered firmly.

"You worry too much." Mama smiled. "We almost home."

Gaucho grunted, "Sure." They still had to change to another subway, and they could wait for what seemed to Gaucho like forever.

Just then a bunch of the crabs started sword fighting. Their claws could be heard striking the stiff paper bag. People sitting nearby looked around puzzled, trying to discover the source of the strange noise.

Wide-eyed and innocent, Gaucho stared straight ahead at the posters advertising L'Eggs pantyhose. For all anyone could tell, he was just sitting there looking bored, with his arms crossed against his chest, staring into space, as his body rocked with the soft rhythm of the subway. His face bore a blank expression.

Suddenly the noise from the bag grew more intense. Gaucho turned his head slightly—and froze!

His mother had slid down to the end of the row and was pretending to read an English newspaper!

8

After the last dead crab carcass was thrown into the garbage and the dishes were washed, Angel and Denise presented Mama and Gaucho with a surprise gift.

"Here. We bought 'em in Miami. Hope you like it." Angel beamed.

"Go ahead, open it." Denise smiled crookedly. Her face was neon red from a deep sunburn, and it was painful for her to talk or smile.

Gaucho tore open his package and found a hard, stiff box with a latch, the kind that comes from jewelry stores. He looked up at Mama excitedly.

"So? Open it." Angel laughed.

Gaucho did. Inside, nestled in the soft blue velvet, was a glistening gold watch with thick gold links for the watchband. He took it carefully out of the box.

"Oh! How beautiful," Gaucho said as Mama helped him snap it on. "I never saw such a beautiful watch. It must have cost a lot of money."

"You like it?" Angel asked.

"Yeah. I sure do," Gaucho said, holding up his wrist to admire it. "Thanks. Thanks a lot."

There was no mistaking that it was an expensive watch, and Gaucho wondered what he could sell it for. Maybe this would be their plane ticket home. He inspected the jewelry box and was happy to see it contained a printed guarantee. He slid the watch off his arm, not wanting to get too attached to it. He placed it carefully in the box.

"I'll save it for special occasions," he told Mama.

Mama was too busy opening her gift to comment. She pried open the cardboard box carefully and uncovered a long, soft, furry lime-green bathrobe.

"I never had anything so beautiful," she said, kissing Angel.

"Denise picked it out," he told her. Mama impulsively moved to kiss Denise, who quickly waved her off. "No! My sunburn!"

"*Gracias.* Both of you." Mama smiled. At Angel's urging she tried the robe on and paraded across the kitchen floor.

"Looks beautiful," they exclaimed.

Mama stood proudly with her hands in the pockets and then she gasped. "What?" Her fingers came up with a fifty-dollar bill.

"For me?"

"Yes, Mama. For you."

Mama started to cry.

Gaucho, who didn't like to see his mother upset, decided to take down the garbage. He picked up the bags and walked out of the apartment, saying, "I'll be right back."

He flew upstairs and knocked on Mario's door.

"Walk me down to the basement."

Mario said, "Okay," and followed him.

Down in the basement, Gaucho dumped the garbage bags into the big aluminum can, and then he and Mario perched themselves on the washing machines. Mario reached behind an overhead pipe and produced an open pack of cigarettes and a soggy pack of matches.

"Damn. The matches are all wet," he said.

"Where can I sell a watch fast?" asked Gaucho.

"I don't know. How would I know?" said Mario, rummaging through the garbage cans. Inside a soggy bag of coffee grounds he found a pack of matches. Some were still dry. He struck one, lit a cigarette, and climbed back on the washing machine. "Who's got a watch to sell?"

"I do. Angel brought me one from Miami, but I'd rather have the money."

Mario passed the cigarette over. Gaucho took a deep puff and pretended to enjoy it.

"How about Blanco?"

Gaucho thought about it, but felt slightly uneasy. "You think so? I heard he's good to buy from—but does he buy too?"

Mario puffed and coughed. "Sure. That's where we bought that radio my father takes to the beach. He got it last year from Blanco, and I know he gave him a camera besides money, so maybe, you know, he buys things too."

Gaucho was hesitant. He knew Blanco from hanging around the neighborhood. He had gone to school with Angel, and they had been on the same softball team. Sometimes he'd see him at the school basketball games. He was always friendly, always cheerful and glad to see you—but something about him was disturbing. His coloring, for one thing, was strange. He was almost a light beige, which is how he came by his nickname. His eyes were a very light green, and his hair was a kinky orange. Nobody knew where he lived or who his parents were. Some said his father was very black and from Africa and his mother very white and blond, which is why he looked the way he did. He also had a knife scar on one cheek and one on the back of his hand, so those alone kept the questioners away. He wasn't someone you bothered. Everyone liked him—but from a distance.

"Maybe I'll go see him tomorrow."

Mario was impressed. "You're gonna talk to Blanco?"

"Why not? I may have something he wants." Gaucho

shook his head and refused a second puff. "And he might pay me for it."

"You never told me what you need the money for." Mario sounded hurt.

"You'll find out sooner or later."

Mario flicked the ashes inside the washing machine. "Well, if you need it, I have $8.47 saved up. You don't even have to tell me what it's for. You can have it."

Gaucho smiled. "Thanks."

They had no trouble finding Blanco the next day. He was in the luncheonette across from school, sitting in the rear booth against the wall.

Not that he was that easy to spot. There was a crowd of people around the booth. Gaucho and Mario looked around timidly, then sat at the counter and ordered sodas. They had to be back in school in half an hour, and from the look of the mob, Blanco was going to be occupied for a long time.

The sodas arrived, and Gaucho and Mario sipped slowly, looking at the booth, waiting for an opportunity to catch Blanco alone.

Gaucho wasn't exactly certain what it was that Blanco did, but he could see that it involved a lot of whispering, smiling, and frozen glances. A person would approach the booth, lean over, and whisper something; Blanco would glance up, nod, and the person would smile and walk away.

"It's got to be drugs," Mario whispered.

"Maybe," Gaucho said, hunched over his soda. He had to attract Blanco's attention soon because he didn't have money to pay for the sodas.

"Or it could be numbers or horse betting . . . or anything." Mario sounded worried.

"That'll be thirty-seven cents each," the man said as he wiped the counter.

Mario looked helplessly at Gaucho, who was sucking the syrup from the bottom of the straw.

"I said—"

"Give us two more," Gaucho said, sliding his glass across the counter. "And put in extra syrup."

The man took the glasses as Gaucho leaped from the stool and headed for the rear booth. He had to have money before the guy came back with the drinks. Gaucho stood back, looking at the circle of people blocking his way, and then boldly pushed his way through till he landed at Blanco's elbow.

"Hey." Blanco smiled. "Where'd you come from?"

Gaucho wedged his body closer. "Have to talk to you," he whispered.

"Sure. You mean right now?"

Gaucho nodded.

Blanco looked at him and grinned. "Okay." He silently waved the mob away, and within seconds it was just he and Gaucho.

"Sit down, Gaucho." He extended his hand, inviting him to share the other side of the booth. "Heard your brother got married. How's he doing?"

"Fine. He's doing fine."

"Good. Next time you see him, give him my regards."

"I will." Gaucho smiled, keeping an anxious eye on the man making the sodas.

"So . . . what's up?"

Gaucho carefully took the plastic jeweler's case out of his jacket and slid it across the Formica tabletop. Blanco picked it up, opened it, glanced at the watch, then closed the box and slid it back to Gaucho.

"Nice watch."

Gaucho smiled. "It's brand new. Never been used. It has a guarantee and everything."

There was an awkward pause. Gaucho leaned forward. "You wanna buy it?"

Blanco chuckled. He edged up his sleeve and exposed a very sleek digital wristwatch with a gold case and diamonds. "I don't need a watch."

Gaucho's heart fell. He could see the counterman approaching. "Here's your soda," he said, plopping it down in front of him. "Your friend says you're paying for both. That'll be—"

"Put it on my bill," Blanco said softly.

"Okay." The counterman smiled. Things were suddenly different. "I put in extra syrup like you said." The man patted Gaucho on the arm. "You want anything else, just call."

Gaucho wiped his sweaty palms on his dungarees. "Thanks."

"Where'd you get the watch?"

"My brother got it in Miami. He gave it to me for a present but I'd rather have the money. I thought maybe . . . since you know so many people . . . maybe . . ."

Blanco reached into his suit pocket and from the lining of the jacket produced a slim leather folder, which Gaucho could see was bulging with money.

"How's thirty?"

Gaucho's eyes sprung open. "Terrific!"

"Okay. I just bought myself a watch I don't need."

Gaucho stuffed the money into his dungaree pocket. "Thanks a lot, Blanco. And for the soda, too. And, listen, if you hear of any jobs, let me know. I already asked everybody but nobody has anything."

Blanco stared at him a long moment. He hadn't noticed how much Gaucho had grown. He was bigger and fuller, and most of the baby look about him was gone. His clothes, his attitude, the way he looked you straight in the eyes—yes, there was a definite change from the little kid he remembered crying on the sidewalk because a car had run over his ball. This kid sitting in front of him didn't look like a crier.

"Ah, listen, Gaucho, you know Mr. Slavin, the science teacher? On the third floor?"

"Oh, sure. I got him Tuesdays and Fridays."

Blanco reached under the table and came up with a long thin box. "You think, ah, when you go back to school now, you can pass by his class and drop this off?" He slid the small box across the table.

"Easy," Gaucho said, stuffing the package in his jacket. "His class is right above mine. No problem."

"I'd appreciate it," Blanco said. He took a bill from his folder and put it in Gaucho's hand. "That's a tip."

"Hey, you don't have to. I'll be glad to do it for free. You did me a favor—I'll do you a favor."

Blanco patted his hand. "Take it."

Gaucho smiled, said, "Okay," and started to leave.

"Listen." Blanco stopped him. "If I happen to find any jobs for you, how do I get in touch with you?"

"Well, I'm always on the block around my house or in the basketball court—or maybe I could just stop in here once a week or something during lunch and see if you have anything."

Blanco nodded. "Yeah. Stop in . . . maybe in a couple of days."

The school bell across the street clanged loudly. The pigeons in the playground fluttered wildly to the top of the chain-link fence.

"Okay. Have to go." Gaucho rushed from the booth and caught up with Mario, who was going out the door.

"Did he buy it?" Mario asked as they dashed up the school steps.

"Yeah. And not only that but he wants me to deliver a package for him and he gave me—" Gaucho hadn't looked at the bill. "Five dollars!"

"Where do you have to deliver it, New Jersey?"

Gaucho laughed. "Naw. Just to the science room."

"Man," Mario mumbled, "I wish I'd asked him for a job."

9

Gaucho rushed home after school and hid the thirty-five dollars in an empty coffee can he kept under his bed. He dumped out the marbles it usually held, replaced the plastic snap-on cover, and rolled the can far under the bed till it was resting against the wall.

He took the calendar from the wall and wrote the number 35 on the back of the last page. Then he circled December 20 and vowed that he and Mama would spend Christmas Day back home. He had a little over three months left. He was confident he could do it.

"Gaucho, put on a nice shirt. We're going to go out," Mama said as she entered the apartment and put the groceries on the table.

He stuck his head out the door. Mama was all dressed up. She was wearing lipstick, and perfume reached him across the room.

"Where we going?"

"To the movies. Come on, hurry up!"

He didn't have to be told twice. Mama quickly put away the groceries as he changed into a clean shirt, and off they went.

If Mama had one true passion in life, it was the movies.

They usually went on the last of the month, when Mama got her check, and it was exciting to go now on the spur of the moment—in the middle of the month.

"You should spend that fifty dollars on yourself and buy something you want," Gaucho told her as they sat on the bus headed downtown.

Mama smiled. "What time is it?"

"I don't know." Gaucho shrugged.

"How come you didn't wear your watch? This is a special occasion, no?"

Gaucho forced a nervous smile. "Yeah . . . but, ah . . . I, ah . . . don't want to wear it to the movies, ah, because it's so dark and what if it falls off? I won't be able to find it."

Mama nodded. "That's smart."

Gaucho relaxed. Mama was busy staring out the window, gazing at the shops and tall buildings. No matter how long she lived in New York, her fascination for the city would never fade.

She and Gaucho could walk down a street they had walked practically every day, and still Mama would find something new and exciting to point out. Gaucho didn't share her enthusiasm, but he enjoyed seeing her happy.

Gaucho glanced at her now as she propped her chin on her hand and stared out the window, a contented glow on her face.

Then a cold fear gripped him. What if she didn't want to go back home?

He pushed the thought away. Hadn't she told him all those stories of her garden where she would water the flowers by moonlight, and how every night after dinner the people would sit on their porches and talk across their rose bushes? She still had all her friends and relatives there. Gaucho figured that she had come to like New York because she had no choice. Mama was always one to make the best of a bad situation. But he knew that deep down, if she really had her choice, Mama would decide to go home.

They rode past a Woolworth's window decorated with Halloween masks and costumes. The sight quickened Gaucho's pulse. After Halloween came Thanksgiving, and before you knew it—Christmas. He'd open his presents this year in Puerto Rico, and that would be the best present of all.

Mama reached up and pulled the cord, which buzzed to her touch. The bus deposited them in front of the movie theater.

They sat in the third row because Mama had trouble understanding all the English, and she liked to study the actors' faces and expressions closely in order to follow the plot.

She and Gaucho shared a large brown grease-stained paper bag filled with homemade popcorn. She had made it while he was in school and kept it warm in the oven. The money she saved by making her own popcorn she spent on ice cream.

For her, America was filled with many delights and astonishing technical accomplishments, but none as extraordinary as the Dixie Cup: a waxed-cardboard container crammed with chocolate and vanilla ice cream. It was all the more enjoyable when eaten with the thin wooden spoon that came with it.

Mama sat happily savoring her ice cream and gazing up at the huge wide screen in the darkened theater. Today they were showing two movies—a western and a war epic about submarines.

Mama preferred movies with lavish costumes, beautiful sets, and exotic backgrounds peppered with singing and dancing. But cowboys and Indians were okay too.

"Look out behind the rock!" Mama warned the unsuspecting sheriff.

Gaucho sank into his seat as people nearby turned to stare. He leaned over and whispered, "Mama, it's only a movie."

Mama smiled and nodded, never taking her eyes from the screen.

The sheriff spun around, whipped out his six-shooter, and drilled the varmint crouching behind the pale rock.

"See? He heard me," Mama said, lapping her ice cream happily.

They stayed for both movies, the cartoons, and the coming attractions. It was dark when they left the theater and went to wait for the bus.

It was Mama who spotted him coming out of the subway station. "Look. There's your teacher. Look." Mama pointed. She recognized him from the recent parents' night when she visited the school and met Gaucho's various teachers.

Gaucho turned and saw Mr. Slavin, carrying his briefcase as he crossed the intersection.

Had Gaucho imagined it, or had the man suddenly changed his course? He seemed to be heading directly their way when he spotted Gaucho and quickly crossed the street.

He probably saw the light changing and decided to take advantage of it.

Gaucho had another surprise when he got home. There was a note slipped under the door addressed to him.

"Call for me when you get home," the note said. It was signed, "Mario."

Mama was pleased. "I never saw two boys be such good friends. It's nice. That's the way it should be."

Gaucho hurried through dinner, dried the dishes, and then fled upstairs, promising to do his homework.

"What's up?" he asked, throwing his books on Mario's

couch. Mario's father was at work in the bakery and his mother was babysitting in an apartment down the hall.

"Where'd you go today?" Mario asked.

"Movies."

"In the middle of the month?"

"Yeah. My mother had money and so we went."

"How come you didn't invite me?"

"We rang your bell. There was nobody home."

Mario nodded. "The ol' witch made me stay after school 'cause she says she can't understand my writing, so she made me write the alphabet on the blackboard fifty times. Do you know that the little q and the capital Z are the hardest letters in the world to write?"

Gaucho stared at his friend with disgust. "Is that what you called me up here to tell me?"

Mario stopped. What did he call him for? "Oh, yeah," he remembered. "When I was walking home I saw Blanco and he told me to tell you to stop by tomorrow at lunch."

Gaucho beamed. "No kidding!"

Mario spread his schoolbooks on the living room floor. He reached up and flipped on the television set. He turned the sound very low in case his mother walked in unexpectedly. She was very strict about not allowing him to watch television until his homework was done.

"I don't like that guy. He makes me nervous," Mario said, referring to Blanco. "Why do you want to work for him anyway? I bet my father could get you a part-

78

time job down at the bakery if I asked him. Like Saturdays."

"Yeah? Doing what? Folding cake boxes? Work a whole day for two dollars? No thanks. I need a lot of money and I need it fast."

Gaucho stretched out on his belly and opened his English book. He knew what was coming next.

"What do you need the money for?"

Gaucho drew in a deep breath. Might as well get it over with. Mario would know eventually.

"I need it to go home. I'm taking Mama back home, and we're gonna be there by Christmas."

Mario's eyes flew open. "Why do you wanna do a dumb thing like that? Spend all that money just to go there for Christmas? Hell! Take the money and buy yourself and your mother and Pachecko and everybody some good presents. Why waste it just to go there for a week? Hell, man, they don't even have any snow. You gonna spend Christmas in a place where everybody is swimming? That's dumb."

Gaucho closed his book. "We're going there to stay."

Mario sat up quickly. "What?"

"That's right. We're going home and we're not coming back."

Mario felt his body jump in various places. His throat suddenly felt dry and thick. "You mean—"

"Let's do our homework." Gaucho turned his attention to the book underneath his chest.

"Right." Mario opened his loose-leaf notebook and took out a clean piece of paper. He wrote his name, the date, his classroom number, and the subject.

The boys lay side by side on the floor as the television flickered silent images above them.

Somehow, they found it difficult to speak.

10

Blanco waved him over. "Hey, my man! What's happening?"

Gaucho slid into the booth. "Oh, not too much."

"Hungry? Here." Blanco pushed a plate of french fries and a cheeseburger across the table. "I haven't touched it. You take it. I'll order another one."

"Okay." Gaucho smiled and started sprinkling the plate, the food, the table, and himself with salt.

"Sid—give us a chocolate shake here," Blanco called across to the counterman.

"Coming!"

"You did good yesterday." Blanco smiled. "You didn't have any trouble, right?"

"No. It was easy. Just walked in the class and gave it to him like you said."

Blanco leaned back and lit up a cigarette. "Right." He exhaled a stream of gray smoke. "Hey. I heard you got a cop in the family."

Gaucho froze. He held the cheeseburger in midair and stared at the pink meat. "Yeah."

Blanco gazed up at the ceiling. "Don't imagine your uncle's too crazy about it. By the way, how is ol' Pachecko?"

"Fine. He's fine." Gaucho attempted to be light. He reached over and took the milkshake the man deposited on the table. He licked the brown foam from the spoon.

"What color Cadillac is he driving this year?" Blanco grinned. "Man, that red one he had last year was a killer! Damn near as big as a fire engine, too, wasn't it?"

Gaucho nodded. "It was big."

"Well, next time you see your uncle, give him my regards."

"Sure."

A group of people—some men and a couple of teen-agers—were sitting on nearby stools, and though their backs were turned to him, Gaucho had the feeling they were waiting for him to leave. He ate more quickly.

"I gotta get back," Gaucho said, wiping his mouth.

"Sure. Ah, listen, you live in the building next to Leon. Right?"

"Yeah."

"Well, ah . . . if it's not too much trouble . . . could you drop something off at his house after school?"

"Sure!" Gaucho's eyes shone. Blanco did have another job for him after all! His feet automatically tapped the floor. He found it hard to be still when he was excited.

"Okay. Tell you what." Blanco reached into his pocket and came up with a plain white envelope. It was the normal thickness of a two-page letter. "On your way home, stop by and give this to Leon. If he isn't home, don't leave it with anyone. Only Leon gets it. Got that?"

"If he's not home, I'll keep going back till I find him," Gaucho said earnestly.

"Okay, baby. You got it!" Blanco reached for his hand and Gaucho felt his fingers close over a small, tightly wadded piece of paper.

The school bell rang. Gaucho picked up his books. "See ya," he said, leaving the restaurant. Behind him he could hear the people on the stools getting up and moving toward the booth.

Gaucho hesitated a moment, wondering if he was supposed to pay for the cheeseburger. The second bell rang, and Gaucho dashed for the school steps. If he owed for the lunch, Blanco could deduct it from his next payment. Gaucho opened his hand and unfolded a five-dollar bill.

At this rate they'd be in Puerto Rico by Thanksgiving.

Mario was waiting outside for him on the steps after school. "You see Blanco?"

"Yeah, he gave me another job." Gaucho quickened his step. "I'm going to drop it off now."

"How much he pay you?"

"Five."

Mario was silent as they walked. When they stopped at the corner for the light, Mario asked casually, "You really serious about going to Puerto Rico?"

"That's right."

Mario glanced down at the ground. "I didn't get no sleep last night." His voice was sad.

"How about a slice of pizza?" Gaucho said, crossing over to a stand.

"I don't have any money." Mario followed quickly.

"So—my treat. Come on." The boys settled at a small table near the jukebox and ordered four slices and two orange drinks.

The prospect of eating brightened Mario a little, but his eyes were still tinged with sadness.

"Listen, we'll write to each other and we can even save up money and call each other once in a while. I bet it doesn't cost that much," Gaucho said.

Mario shrugged. "I never have any money. How am I going to save up?"

Gaucho thought about that. "Hey! I know! When I leave you can take over my job with Blanco. You'll make a lot of money!"

Mario sat up quickly. "You think so? You think he'd give me the job?"

"Why not? In fact, just before I leave, I'll let you go on some deliveries with me so he gets used to seeing you, and then you just take over. Okay?"

"God! That would be wonderful. Maybe I can even make enough to give my mother some money. Down where Papa works they cut out all the overtime, so he doesn't make as much money as he used to, and Mama says it's going to be like that for a long time."

A young boy delivered the four slices and the drinks to the table. Gaucho picked up the square piece of wax paper holding the triangle slice of crust, tomato sauce, and bubbling brown-singed cheese. He sprinkled the slice, the table, and his lap with salt. Then he shook the bottle of tiny red peppers over the pizza. By the time Gaucho was finished, Mario had already eaten his first slice.

When they finally left, they both found it hard to walk quickly. They took their time getting home. Four slices, two drinks, and an Italian ice each.

Gaucho paused at the stoop to Leon's building. "He *would* live on the fourth floor," he groaned. Mario elected to hold Gaucho's books and wait for him on the stoop. He sat down and rubbed his belly. The pizza felt good going down, but once it got there it just laid around and rumbled.

Gaucho returned wearily a few minutes later.

"No one was home. I'll have to come back later."

Mario got up and they entered their own building. "What do you think is in the envelope, anyway?"

"How do I know? Must be something important to be worth five dollars."

"Let me see it," said Mario.

"Okay, but be careful." Gaucho took the envelope from between the pages of his science book.

Mario turned it over in his hand and felt the weight of it. "Looks like a letter, huh? Why didn't he just put a stamp on it and mail it?"

"Who knows?"

"Look," said Mario, "one of the flaps is loose. I bet we could open it real easy and then glue it back, and nobody would know."

"Give me that." Gaucho whipped the envelope out of Mario's chubby hand.

"Don't you want to know what's in it? Maybe it's stolen goods or government secrets or maybe—"

"It's not my business. And you keep your mouth shut."

Mario looked disappointed. "You mean you ain't curious or nothing? Not even a little bit?"

Gaucho headed toward his apartment. "Look. My job is just like a mailman's. I get paid to deliver packages and mail. You know what happens to a mailman if he opens a letter? He gets sent to jail."

Mario called, "Yeah, but some other people can go to jail just for delivering—if they're delivering something that's wrong. You know what I mean?"

Gaucho ran up the stairs. "See you later," he yelled, and threw open the door to his apartment.

"I'm home, Mama."

"Hi, Gaucho."

He stopped short. There was Jimmy Raddigan, in his uniform, sitting at the kitchen table.

"Hello."

"Your mother went down to get some milk. She'll be right back."

Gaucho nodded, slinked past the table, and went into his room, where he quickly drew the curtain closed.

"I got tickets to a hockey game for tonight," Jim called to him. "Wanna go?"

"Sure!" Gaucho said quickly—and then wished he hadn't.

"Great. After dinner, we'll drive to my place and I'll change clothes, and then we'll go to the game."

Gaucho crawled under the bed, took out the coffee can, and put in a dollar bill and eighty-five cents in change. He rolled the can deep under the bed and camouflaged it behind some dirty socks and T-shirts. He then went to the last page of the calendar and wrote down the new total: $36.85.

He heard Mama open the front door, and he quickly replaced the calendar.

"Gauchito? You home?"

"Yes, Mama."

Gaucho took the envelope, placed it carefully in his science book, and put the book under his pillow. What if Mario was right? What if there was something stolen or illegal in the envelope, and there he was with a cop sitting in his kitchen?

"Gaucho's going to the game with me," Jimmy said as he helped Mama put the groceries away.

"Good. Then I can go to Carmela's house and watch my *novelas*." She smiled. Mama enjoyed the Spanish programs on TV, which she couldn't get on her old set, since it didn't have a UHF antenna.

Jimmy had come to visit a few times since the wedding, and it was obvious that Mama liked his company. Once Gaucho came home and found him hanging out over the windowsill polishing the window. Usually he stopped by for an hour or so on his way to work, but today he looked like he was settled in for a long visit.

Jimmy just naturally liked kids. They amused him. They were fun to be with. You could relax and didn't have to pretend to be anything you weren't. Even while in high school, Jimmy had helped coach a Little League team and a Pee Wee basketball squad. He would have been a teacher except he didn't like the idea of being cooped up in a classroom all day.

He had liked Gaucho the first moment they met. There was something very honest and proud about the boy that appealed to him. And smart. He could see it. There was also an underlying sadness in Gaucho that Jimmy could relate to. When he thought back to his own childhood, very little of it was pleasant. He was too shy to be popular and too sickly to play sports. In a way, Gaucho reminded him of himself.

Mama pulled aside the curtain. "If you're going with Jimmy, you better do your homework now."

"I did it in school."

"Then you can help me with dinner. Jimmy is going to stay, and I'm gonna make his favorite, yellow rice and chicken. You can cut up the bananas."

Gaucho groaned. "I promised Mario I'd help him fix his skates." Mario didn't have any skates, but it was the first thing that came to mind.

"Let him go out. I'll help you," Jimmy told Mama. "I want to learn how to cook anyway. I'm getting pretty tired of frozen dinners."

While Mama protested that Jimmy was company and therefore should just sit and be waited on—and while Jimmy countered that if he was still considered "company" he might just as well go out to some luncheonette—Gaucho grabbed his science book and beat it out the door. "See ya."

"Be back at five," his mother yelled.

Gaucho was running up the stairs to Leon's apartment when he spotted Leon coming down.

"Hi. I got something for you." Gaucho took the envelope carefully out of the book. "It's from Blanco."

Leon looked at him suspiciously. "How come he gave it to you?"

Gaucho smiled proudly. "'Cause I work for him."

"Is that so?" Leon tore open the envelope.

"Any answer for Blanco?"

"No, that's okay." Leon dug into his pockets. "Here." He flipped Gaucho a quarter.

"Thanks. See ya." Gaucho ran downstairs and into the street.

Leon leaned against the wooden banister and read the note: "This is a test run. Examine the envelope closely and sniff it to see if new glue has been used. Check and see if it has been opened. This is the kid's second job for me. I'm thinking of making him a regular. Let me know."

Leon turned over the envelope, examined it closely. Except for a dab of what appeared to be pizza sauce, it looked legitimate.

He wasn't sure whether hiring Gaucho was a good idea. The word had spread quickly about his having a cop in the family. Still, if you looked at it another way . . . maybe having a cop as a relative wasn't so bad. Especially if he could be convinced to cooperate.

Leon stuck the envelope in his jacket pocket and decided to visit Blanco. Gaucho would get an A.

11

On the way to school the next morning, Mario was filled with questions. "You mean just the two of you went out together for the whole night?"

Gaucho nodded. "First he drove me to his apartment in Greenwich Village—you should see his dog, a German shepherd, it's bigger than the apartment—and then he changed into regular clothes and we stopped at the precinct 'cause he had to pick up the tickets for the game. He left them in his locker."

Mario stopped abruptly. "You went inside a police station?"

Gaucho laughed. "Yeah. You should've been there. It was just like the movies. There was this woman crying 'cause somebody stole her purse, and then there was this old lady who was yelling 'cause she had no heat or hot water, and then they had a man who was arrested for fighting with a bus driver. He wouldn't pay or something. I don't know. He was sitting there waiting for his lawyer."

"And what were you doing all this time?"

"I went into the locker room with Jimmy and he introduced me to the other cops. They were sitting around playing cards—one guy was polishing his shoes. Everybody said hello. They were okay—for cops. Then Jimmy got the tickets and we went to the hockey game."

Mario was silent for a few blocks. Then, as they approached the school, he blurted out sadly, "Sounds like you had a good time with that cop."

Gaucho smiled. "Yeah, I guess so. Do you know that when he was in the Navy he was stationed in San Juan? That's how come he likes the food so much. He was there for nine months and he knows a lot of the places that Mama knows. That's what we were talking about at dinner. He really liked it down there."

"Well, maybe you can all move down there with the spiders and the snakes and the mosquitoes and live happy together forever," Mario shot back.

"What the hell is wrong with you?" Gaucho felt his anger rising. "So I went to a hockey game. Big deal. I have to take you everyplace I go? You went to the Bronx Zoo two times this summer. Did I get mad?"

"I went with relatives—I didn't go with no lousy cop!" Mario leaned over and confronted him nose to nose.

"Well, that lousy cop happens to be a relative!" Gaucho yelled—their noses almost touching.

Maybe it was the absurdity of the remark or the way they looked—glaring and growling at each other—but suddenly, standing there like two statues while throngs of students rushed past them, the whole scene just seemed ridiculous.

Gaucho and Mario started laughing. They laughed till they reached the second floor and went into their separate classrooms. They parted with a friendly wave.

They didn't see each other again till the last period, when both classes met in the science room. At the final bell, when everyone was rushing for the door, Mr. Slavin called Gaucho aside.

"Gaucho, I've been meaning to tell you how pleased I am with your marks. Your work is excellent. There are still a few formulas and theories that confuse you, but overall you're doing very good work." The man smiled.

"Thanks." Gaucho shifted his books from one arm to the other.

"Ah, Gaucho . . . I, ah . . . guess you know that I run a photography class after school twice a week. We meet in the audio-visual room, and I show slides that I or some of the students have taken. And we go on field trips to take pictures. When the weather gets warm, we might spend a day on the Staten Island Ferry or visit the Statue of Liberty. . . ."

Gaucho continued smiling, though his legs were getting tired. He glanced outside the door and could see Mario waiting impatiently for him.

"Do you have any hobbies?"

Gaucho looked at the teacher, looked at his books,

looked at the ceiling. "No." He said it softly. Almost ashamed. His palms started to sweat.

"I think every young boy should have a hobby of some sort. Not only is it educational, but it keeps the mind and the body usefully occupied," Mr. Slavin said seriously.

Gaucho nodded and shifted his weight.

"What do you do after school?" The smile on the teacher's face was gone.

Gaucho shrugged. "I go to the store for my mother, I do my homework—and if it's still light out, I play."

Mr. Slavin pondered this a moment. "Gaucho, normally I wouldn't care, except you are a fine student. You have a good mind and a good attitude. I wouldn't want that to change."

Gaucho didn't know if he was being complimented or punished. It was hard to tell by the nervous tremor he felt coming from the teacher.

"A hobby also fills time and keeps people from perhaps making the wrong friendships. Do you know what I mean?" His voice lowered to almost a whisper.

Gaucho stared at him. "But I don't have a camera."

Just then another teacher came in. "I need a ride home with you. Okay?"

Mr. Slavin smiled. "Sure." He turned his attention back to Gaucho. "Just think about what I said."

"Okay." Gaucho fled the room.

"What was that all about?" asked Mario.

"I'm not sure," said Gaucho. "I think he's trying to sell me a camera."

In the weeks that followed, Gaucho was kept too busy to think of joining any classes. Armando's relatives moved to Miami as soon as the first cold weather struck, and Gaucho became his new delivery boy, after school and all day Saturdays.

Since it was now late October and it got dark early, Gaucho had to be home by five. He made his deliveries on a big heavy bicycle with a steel basket on the front large enough to hold a crate. Sometimes Mario helped him and they split the tips. Or Mario would watch the delivery bike while Gaucho lugged the cartons up to the apartments.

Gaucho was also making deliveries for Blanco once or twice a week. It usually was a small package, sometimes just a thick envelope, and generally to be delivered to neighborhood people he had seen around but didn't really know. Now it seemed that he knew everyone.

Mama had let him have the grocery job as long as it didn't interfere with his schoolwork. How he chose to spend the money he made was strictly up to him. Mama did not interfere or make suggestions. She knew her son well enough to know he would not be foolish with the money.

The first payment Gaucho received from Armando was in a small brown envelope with his name on it. He was paid by the hour for delivery work and by the job when he swept, dusted the stock, or bagged groceries.

His first pay envelope contained $14.72. That didn't include the $7.25 he had made in tips from the people who ordered the groceries.

It was the proudest moment of his life when he came home with his own pay envelope, opened it at the kitchen table—and handed Mama ten dollars. "For you." He smiled. It felt wonderful.

Mama reached out slowly and took the money. "*Gracias,* Gauchito," she said as she tried to stop the tears that sprang to her eyes.

"Don't," he warned her.

Mama smiled and hugged him close. "No mother ever had a better son," she said.

He could imagine how she would carry on the day he revealed they were going home. There would be no stopping the tears that day.

. It was soon Halloween night, and Gaucho was having his first party ever. It had been Mama's idea. They had never before been able to afford even a birthday party, but with the extra money that Gaucho was bringing home, Mama decided that he deserved a special celebration. He was entitled to some fun.

For the past weeks she had seen him come home exhausted every day, and a few times he even fell asleep at the table doing his homework. She had even started hinting that maybe he was doing too much . . . maybe he should only work a few days . . . but then she would see the new gloves and the new winter jacket that she couldn't afford to buy him.

So, instead, Mama decided he would have a party, and she would pay for it out of the money he had given her.

Mama got up early that morning, and as soon as Gaucho left for school she started baking the two chocolate cakes she'd decorate with orange icing.

All week long Gaucho had been passing out invitations at school, and he expected anywhere from one to forty kids. He purposely invited a lot in case only a few showed up. It was his first party, and he wanted to be certain that at least someone would show up. One thing was definite: whoever came would have to wear a costume. Any kind was allowed—homemade, secondhand, bought, borrowed. . . .

It was Mama's idea to give a prize to the one wearing the best costume. She bought a present, carefully wrapped it, and hid it from Gaucho. "Only the winner opens it," she announced.

"What if I have the best costume? If you pick me, everybody will say the contest was fixed. Just because it's my party doesn't mean I shouldn't have a chance to win just like anybody else. Right?"

Mama listened and agreed with his logic. She solved the dilemma the next day by getting Uncle Pachecko to serve as judge.

"Your uncle will be here for the party and he will pick."

Gaucho was elated. Everyone knew Pachecko to be honest, so when he won it would be fair and square and no one could be angry.

Now—to devise a costume that would be a sure winner!

For days Gaucho had tried to learn what Mario was planning to wear, but his friend was being unusually mysterious. Gaucho even enlisted the aid of his mother.

"Ask Mario's mother," he suggested strongly. "She's your best friend. She'll tell you."

Mama came back and reported, "She won't say nothing. I tried."

On the day of the party, while Gaucho was in school and the cakes were baking, Mama and Mario's mother, Señora Cabrera, decorated the kitchen and living room with streamers of orange and black paper. Pictures of witches, skeletons, and ghosts were glued to the windows and the front door. A big, fat jack-o'-lantern of crinkly orange tissue paper sat in the center of the kitchen table, surrounded by colorful plastic plates, knives, forks, and cups.

Mama cooked two large pots of popcorn, and Señora Cabrera made two dozen candied apples. Pachecko had said he would bring a couple of gallons of ice cream, plus pretzels, potato chips, and beer.

"The party is for children. They do not drink beer," Mama had told her brother-in-law over the phone.

"Who said anything about the kids? The beer is for us. We have our own party." He laughed.

Mama thanked him and reminded him that she didn't drink. "Just be here on time. And sober."

Now, with the apartment decorated with streamers, floating witches, and goblins, Mama and her weary friend sat down to blow up the pile of balloons.

"After all this, I don't think I have any breath." Señora Cabrera smiled.

"Drink the coffee. It gives you strength," Mama answered.

It was nice sitting in the toasty kitchen, enjoying the good warm smells from the oven while the temperature outside was a frosty thirty-three degrees. The radiator in the kitchen coughed contentedly as the steam heat rose through the pipes; outside, the wind howled against the windows.

Mama touched the soft mountain of balloons.

"Cari," she confessed to her friend, "I never had a party."

The other woman nodded. "Me either. Who had the money for such things?"

Mama smiled. "I always wanted a party. And I know it hurt my mama that she couldn't give me one. But every time I asked, she used to tell me, 'Someday, Maria. Someday.' But somehow, someday never came." She looked around at the table, the walls, the windows, and said proudly, "This will be our party, too."

The alarm clock went off, and Mama rushed to the oven to remove the cakes.

The hours flew, and before long Gaucho was running through the door with his books.

"Mama!" He ran excitedly through the apartment, utterly astounded, trying to look at everything at once. "Mama! It's beautiful." He ran over and kissed her, almost knocking her into the bowl of orange icing.

"Be careful, *hijo*." She laughed.

"I never saw anything so beautiful. You did all this by yourself?"

Before she could answer, he ran out of the apartment and dashed back in, dragging a huffing, out-of-breath Mario.

"How about that!" Gaucho stood back and let his friend experience the sight.

Mario's large round eyes expanded. "Damn!"

Mama tapped the stovetop firmly with her wooden spoon, which meant, "Watch your language."

But Mario was too overwhelmed. "Damn."

Gaucho quickly hustled him out. "See you at seven."

Then Gaucho ran into his room, whipped the curtain closed, quickly changed out of his school clothes, and ran out buttoning his new jacket and slipping on his gloves.

"Where you going?" Mama asked, somewhat annoyed.

"To work." He headed for the door.

Mama grabbed his arm. "I thought you were going to help me get things ready. There's still a lot to do—the balloons, the furniture has to be moved—"

Gaucho struggled to get free. "Mama. I tried to get the day off, but with the cold weather everybody is ordering the groceries by phone and Armando has ten orders already piled up. Don't worry. The party doesn't start till seven. I'll be home by five."

"But . . . but. . . ."

Gaucho hopped on his tiptoes and kissed Mama firmly on the cheek. "See ya," he said, yanked free, and dashed down the stairs.

Mama mumbled to herself in Spanish and went back to her cakes.

The next two hours sped by quickly. Cari and Mario helped Mama rearrange furniture and finish decorating.

Gaucho pedaled the bike back to the store after delivering his last order. His legs were hurting from pedaling against the wind. His arms ached from gripping the icy handlebars tightly. He thought seriously of quitting the job, but as always, when such thoughts presented themselves, he instantly dismissed them. He knew he'd feel better as soon as he rested.

Armando watched with growing satisfaction as Gaucho wheeled the heavy bike though the store and into the back room.

"Tough night out there, huh?"

Gaucho drew the warm air into his chest hungrily. "Yeah," he answered. He was almost afraid to ask, but he did anyway. "Is it always this busy? I mean, in winter?"

Armando smiled. "It's my best time of the year. Everyone is too cold to leave the apartment, so they call!"

Gaucho groaned.

"Listen, if you want, get somebody to help you. You know, you work a couple of days and then the other guy works a couple of days . . . you can do that. That's what my son used to do when he had the job. He said it was too much for one person every day."

It sounded tempting, and Gaucho knew he wouldn't have any trouble finding someone. Not Mario, though. He refused to climb stairs carrying packages. But there were plenty of others.

"Naw, it's all right," Gaucho told him. "I'll keep it the way it is. I need the money."

"Okay, *amigo*. You're the boss."

"I'll sweep tomorrow night extra good. I gotta go right home." Gaucho paused at the door. "I'm having a party." He waved and ran out of the store.

Outside, parked next to the curb, was a long, dark car. As Gaucho rushed past, bent against the wind, Blanco opened the passenger door.

"Hey. Gaucho."

Gaucho stopped and spun around. "Hi!" He smiled.

"Get in." Blanco held the door open. Gaucho jumped in quickly, eager to accept the warmth of the car. It would be a real luxury to get a ride home, even for two blocks.

"I want you to do me a little favor," Blanco said as he slid back behind the steering wheel. "Okay?" He smiled underneath his dark glasses. It was impossible to see his eyes.

Gaucho sensed a kind of urgency. His instinct was to get out of the car.

"I'm sorry. I can't. I have to go straight home." He smiled, trying the friendly approach. "I'm having a party tonight and I have to help my mother." Gaucho stopped. He thought he sounded like a baby. He could tell by the silence that Blanco wasn't too happy. Maybe he was regretting ever having hired him.

"What I had in mind isn't going to take long. At most, twenty minutes. I could do it myself, but I figured you could use the work. I didn't know that all of a sudden you was a rich guy. That's okay. If you don't need the twenty bucks—you don't need it. I'll see ya." Blanco leaned across Gaucho's lap and opened the passenger door.

The cold wind ripped through the car. Gaucho sat motionless.

"You sure just twenty minutes?" Gaucho sat next to the open door.

"Maybe half an hour. Shouldn't be more."

"Can I call my mother and tell her?"

"Sure. I'll stop at a phone." Blanco told him.

Gaucho reached out and pulled the car door closed. "Okay. Let's go."

Blanco eased the car away from the curb and steered it toward Broadway. He reached over, pressed in the cigarette lighter, waited a few seconds for it to pop out, and then lit his long, thin brown cigar.

"Your birthday?" he asked, exhaling a sweet, thick smoke.

"No. Why?"

"Nothing. You said you were having a party."

Gaucho laughed. "Halloween party."

"Oh." Blanco smiled. He reached under the seat and came up with a tape, which he inserted into the player mounted under his dashboard. Loud trumpets and bugles invaded the car. Gaucho jumped. The sound was shooting at him from all angles.

"I'm crazy about bullfighting music," Blanco admitted.

Gaucho looked around, up and down. "How many speakers do you have?"

"Six." Blanco smiled proudly. "The guy who installed it said it's never been done before—not in a car. He had to invent a whole special thing to get it to work. Terrific, huh?"

Gaucho couldn't hear a word that was said because of the blaring trumpets. He assumed he'd been asked a question, so he smiled broadly and nodded. It seemed to satisfy Blanco, who with his free hand was playing the dashboard as if it were a bongo.

It came as a relief when Blanco slowed the car to the curb and pointed to the outside telephone booth.

"Be right back," Gaucho yelled. It was great to be outside with only the taxis, buses, ambulances, and police sirens to contend with. Gaucho took a dime from his dungarees pocket and dialed Señora Cabrera's number.

It was dark, and the neon lights on the street were ablaze. The cold wind whipped across his legs and face. He covered one ear with the telephone receiver and the other with his gloved hand. A gust of wind sent a sheet of newspaper dancing in the air.

Gaucho heard the phone ringing. He counted the rings—five . . . six . . . seven. Mario usually picked it up on the first ring. His mother took a little longer and his father, if he was home, never picked it up because he said it never was for him anyway. Eleven . . . twelve . . . thirteen. . . . Where the hell could they be? This was the time for Mario's mother to be cooking dinner, and Mario wasn't allowed out after dark.

Maybe he dialed the wrong number. Gaucho hung up, waited for the click—and lost his money.

He punched the phone. "You goddamn thief!"

He took off his glove and searched for another dime. He found two nickels and deposited them in the slot.

He shot a helpless glance at Blanco, who didn't notice him. Blanco was relaxed, leaning back and listening to his music.

Gaucho dialed and listened to the familiar ringing. His stomach tensed. If he couldn't get Mama to tell her he would be late, he'd get into a lot of trouble. He would probably be punished and made to stay in for a week. Mama was very strict about being home on time. Six . . . seven . . . eight. . . . Still, he had a good excuse. He did call—twice! It wasn't his fault if they weren't home. Where the hell were they? Maybe the phone was out of order.

Gaucho hung up. He waited for the money to fall, heard a hollow click—and lost his money again. He punched the phone and hurried into the car.

"Nobody home."

Blanco nodded and eased the car into the flow of traffic.

"There was nobody home," Gaucho yelled over the music. "I better get home fast or my mother's going to be worried."

"We'll be back in no time," Blanco said. He pressed the gas pedal, and the car vibrated and shot forward, leaving the other traffic behind.

Gaucho sat huddled near the door, biting his fingernails. It was only about twenty after five, and once this week he'd been at the store till six o'clock. Mama had come down to find him and found him sweeping behind the counter. He had been so busy he'd forgotten the time. Seeing him there, Mama had been too relieved to yell. She even stopped to chat with some of the customers whom she knew from the neighborhood. Armando apologized for keeping her son so late and gave her a day-old but still fresh peach pie to take home.

Maybe she would think he was working late again and not worry, Gaucho thought. He was certain of one thing—he would have to be home by six, because if his mother went to the store looking for him and he wasn't there . . .

He remembered that something bad had happened in the family once—a sickness or a death—and Mama had become so upset that she suffered one of her asthma attacks and had to be rushed to the hospital. It was the longest week of his life till she came home.

If she went to the store and didn't find him there . . . He was too frightened to think about it. He could always try calling Mario's again.

He wondered if Blanco would mind making another stop to let him use the phone. Maybe there was a phone where they were going. Gaucho looked out the window, searching in the lighted shops for a clock. The car was going too fast for him to read the time. Finally, Blanco stopped at a red light and Gaucho read the clock hanging on the wall of a barbershop. It was 5:23.

A new thought came to Gaucho. He stared ahead out the windshield and wondered if Blanco had sold the watch Gaucho had sold him.

12

It was 5:25 as Mama closed the living room window. She rubbed her cold arms and went into the kitchen, where Señora Cabrera was taping balloons to the wall.

"I don't see him coming," Mama said, looking worried.

"He probably had to work late again. You know how lazy that Armando is. He don't do nothing in that store except smile and flirt with the women. I wouldn't go in that store if I was starving. I'd rather walk the two blocks and go to the supermarket, where nobody knows nobody and you get your food and go home. No skinny bag of bones has to tell me I look pretty. I know when I look pretty. I don't need no fresh mouth to tell me."

Mama handed her friend some more balloons.

"You know why his relatives moved to Miami? Huh? Because Armando was getting too friendly with one of the daughters. Only sixteen. But big—she make two of us. Armando's wife found out, and all of them were on the bus to Miami the next day." She glanced at her friend, who still looked uncertain. "Don't worry. He be home soon."

Mama smiled and pitched in to help decorate, but every once in a while—if she heard the least little sound—she'd stop and cock her head toward the door.

Mario huffed and puffed his way into the kitchen. "I got rid of the garbage. I'm going upstairs to put on my costume."

His mother yelled down from the ladder, "First you take a bath. You don't put clean clothes on a dirty body." Mario started to protest. "Just do it!" his mother ordered.

Mario mumbled angrily to himself and headed for the door. "I'll be the only one at the party who smells like soap." He slammed the door behind him.

The women looked at each other and laughed. Mama was still smiling when she went into the living room and opened the window. She leaned out as far as she could. The dark streets were empty. She could see the traffic light two blocks ahead on Broadway and the slow stream of cars emitting gray smoke from their exhaust pipes. Very few people were walking around in the cold air. On the corner were a man and his dog. The dog sniffed the gutter while the man waited for the light to change. A woman hurried below with her shopping cart filled with groceries. Across the street, a fat striped cat jumped at the garbage can and sent it sprawling on its side, spilling most of its contents on the sidewalk.

Mama stared down the block as long as her cold face

and arms could withstand the icy air. Then she closed the window and warmed herself beside the kitchen radiator.

The bullfight music mercifully came to an end, and while Blanco drove, fumbling underneath the seat with one hand to retrieve a new tape, Gaucho asked him, "Can I try to call the house again?"

Blanco pulled up to the curb. Gaucho knew he was annoyed, but didn't care. It was getting close to six and they still weren't wherever they were going.

Gaucho jumped out of the car, slammed the door, and took a dime from his pocket as he ran to the phone. He deposited the dime—his last one—and quickly dialed. The phone rang. Gaucho paced up and down as far as the wire phone cord would let him—which was about six inches. Four . . . five . . . six. . . . He stared at the digital clock above the bank on the corner. It was 5:52. His stomach tightened. He should never have agreed to go with Blanco. Nine . . . ten . . . eleven. Gaucho prayed that if God let someone answer the phone, Gaucho would never go on another job for Blanco again—ever. He would quit his job right then—right there!

Mario was sitting in the tub of hot water in the kitchen watching a rerun of "Star Trek." Captain Kirk was yelling at his crew on the Starship *Enterprise* and his commands drowned out the persistently ringing phone. Mario lathered up and sank his homemade submarine—two clothespins tied together.

Gaucho got back into the car reluctantly. Not only was he in a lot of trouble, but his mother would probably call off the party. He stared glumly out the window as Blanco drove on.

"Okay. We're there," Blanco whispered finally.

Gaucho sat up straight. There was no mistaking where they were as he looked out the window at the brightly lit shops, restaurants, and stores with the strange, pretty writing. They were in Chinatown. Gaucho had never been there before, but he'd heard of it. He had never seen so many Chinese people all at once. The area was alive with parents, children, old men, and teenagers, all laughing, running, and walking through the narrow streets blazoned with neon colors. It looked like Christmas.

Blanco maneuvered the car through narrow streets and alleys, sometimes even driving up on the sidewalk to avoid the mounds of cartons of garbage lined up on the curb behind the restaurants. It seemed as if there were twenty restaurants on every block, and many had people lined up on the sidewalk waiting to get in.

Gaucho saw an outdoor phone booth and exclaimed, "Look!" Blanco jammed on the brakes. Gaucho laughed. He had never seen a phone booth in the shape of a pagoda. The enclosed phone was topped by a red and gold dome that reminded him of the Chinese temples he had seen in his geography books.

"Hurry up," Blanco snarled.

Gaucho realized that Blanco thought he wanted to make

a phone call. He took advantage of the opportunity and jumped from the car. He put in the dime and listened again to the familiar ring. Three . . . four—

"Hello?"

"Mario? Is that you?"

"Yeah. Who's this?"

"Me. Gaucho! Where the hell was everybody? I've been calling for an hour," he said, his heart pounding.

"I've been downstairs taking out your lousy garbage. Where are you? The party's going to start soon."

"Never mind. I'll be home soon. I had to do something. Look. Run downstairs and tell my mother I'll be home in half an hour. Half an hour. No more. All right?"

Mario groaned. "Man, I just got out of the tub. All I got on is my underwear and socks."

Gaucho told him very firmly and precisely, "Knock on the floor. Right now. Come on. Let me hear it!"

"Okay." Mario put the phone on the floor and banged on the linoleum with the broom handle.

Downstairs, Mama was leaning out the window when her friend pulled her in. "Telephone, Maria, telephone. The floor." She pointed to the ceiling.

Mama grabbed her broom and banged twice, which was the signal that she was coming.

"She's on her way up," Mario said into the phone.

"Okay. I can't wait. Just tell Mama I'm doing a favor for somebody and I'll be home in half an hour. Got that?"

"Got it."

"Okay. Bye." Gaucho hung up.

He felt good. He took his time walking to the car. He looked around the small, strange neighborhood. He had never seen such an exciting place with so many people. The hot aroma of exotic foods conspired for his attention.

A Chinese baker in a white hat and apron stood inside his shop, placing trays of tiny colorful cakes in his window. He glanced up at Gaucho and smiled, revealing his missing teeth. Gaucho smiled back.

"Get in the car!" Blanco shouted.

Gaucho jumped. For a moment he had forgotten. He threw open the door and jumped in. "Sorry."

"You never been here before?"

"No," Gaucho said, trying to conceal his excitement.

"Do the job good, I bring you back one night and we'll go in one of these places and have dinner. Okay?"

"Okay." He tried to act bored, but inside his pulse was racing. Probably no one in his whole family had ever been here before or seen anything like it. Someday he would bring Mama and show her.

"We're getting close now," Blanco said, slowing the car. It was obvious he knew the narrow alleys very well. "Around the corner, on the left, is a playground. Got two basketball courts and some swings. In between the basketball courts is a small bench. There's gonna be a woman sitting there. She's gonna have a shopping bag." He reached over behind his seat and, steering with one hand, produced a shopping bag, which he placed on the seat between him and Gaucho. "The shopping bag will look like this one."

Gaucho eyed the bag. It was bright yellow with red flowers and said "A&P."

"I'm gonna drop you off here. You walk to the corner, turn left, go the playground. You go up to the bench. Put the shopping bag down. Lean over like you gotta tie your shoelace, and then pick up her shopping bag and walk away. Then you walk down the block—you'll see the subway and a florist on the corner—and I'll pick you up there."

Gaucho looked at the shopping bag and bit his lip nervously.

"You got it? Any questions?"

"I don't think so," Gaucho said, chewing the inside of his mouth.

"Just put this bag down and pick up the other one. Don't say nothing to nobody. Just keep walking." Blanco slid the shopping bag against Gaucho's body. "Okay, man, it's all yours."

Gaucho nodded and opened the car door. He slid the bag off the seat and almost dropped it in the gutter. He was unprepared for its heavy weight. He thought he saw Blanco wince as he pulled away in the car.

Gaucho grabbed the bag with both hands and walked to the corner. The string handles cut into his skin. He wondered how the unknown woman would be able to lift it.

He suddenly became scared. What if Blanco drove off without him? How would he get home from Chinatown? What if none of the Chinese people spoke any English? Maybe they hated Puerto Ricans!

Gaucho wanted to drop the bag and run, but he had nowhere to run to.

Gaucho spotted the playground across the street. It was empty except for a drunk sleeping on the ground near the seesaw. Gaucho hoped he was drunk, not dead. He was used to seeing drunks lying on the sidewalk in his neighborhood, but here in this strange place it scared him.

He spotted the old Chinese woman sitting on the bench. She was sitting slightly away from the lamppost, so he couldn't see her face too well, but he knew from the way she was hunched over—huddled inside her dark coat—that she was old. Her head was covered with a dark scarf and he noticed she was wearing rubber boots.

His hands started to ache. He switched the shopping bag to his other side and approached the bench slowly. He glanced behind him. No one was following him. He glanced down the block as far as he could see. He could see the entrance to the subway station and the bright yellow florist sign, but no black car and no driver. He looked at the drunk, who was unconscious on the ground, and hoped someone would help him soon before he froze to death.

Gaucho was a few feet from the bench when he spotted the old woman's shopping bag. It was at the end of the bench on the ground, sitting between her and a wire trash basket. Gaucho inhaled deeply and walked toward the woman. Her head was twisted to the side as if she were asleep.

Gaucho stopped a few inches in front of her and crouched down to tie his shoelaces. He put his shopping bag near her feet and took his time tying his shoes, all the while glancing at her bag. He sneaked a look at the woman inches away under the lamplight and then realized she was really asleep. Her eyes were closed and he could hear her heavy breathing.

He was frightened. What if she was the wrong woman? What if she was just someone who had gone shopping at the A&P and sat down on the bench to rest and had fallen asleep? It was logical. It could have happened that way. What if he touched her shopping bag and she woke up and started screaming?

Gaucho's hands trembled. The laces tangled in his fingers. Maybe Blanco had made a mistake? His knees touched the cold pavement and the wind crept under his cuffs into his pants legs.

"Hurry up! Get out of here!"

Gaucho's heart stopped! He looked around quickly. He looked at the old woman. Her face was still twisted to one side and her eyes were closed. Then she opened one eye and fixed it on him.

"Leave it and go. Tell Blanco to be careful. They've been watching me. Go. Hurry."

The woman was whispering, but in Gaucho's hysteria it sounded as if the entire world could hear. His chest pounded with fear. He felt his neck tighten.

Gaucho swallowed hard and stood straight. He brushed off his pants leg, walked past the old lady, and swung his arm. It connected with the shopping bag, which dangled lightly from his hand as he lifted it.

"Hold it right there!"

Gaucho spun around. The drunk had leaped to his feet, bounded over the seesaw, and had his hand on the old lady's shoulder. With his other hand he reached into his pocket, took out a silver whistle, and blew it.

"Don't move!" he ordered Gaucho.

The old lady lurched forward, grabbed the heavy shopping bag, and swung it against the man's legs.

"Run, stupid!" she yelled. "Run!"

The man stumbled and made a grab for Gaucho as he fell. Gaucho sprang from his reach, the man's fingers coming within inches of snaring the hood on his jacket.

Three men in suits and overcoats leaped from a parked car and ran into the playground.

"Run!" the old lady screamed again.

Gaucho took off. One of the men had the exit blocked. In a flash—without even thinking—Gaucho made a leap and laced his fingers in the chain-link fence. He dug the toes of his sneakers deep into the fence as he propelled his body upward.

"Get him!" One of the men pointed to Gaucho.

Gaucho flung himself over the top of the fence and landed with a thud on the sidewalk below. He quickly scampered to his feet and realized to his amazement that he was still holding on to the shopping bag. Panic had frozen his fingers over the handle.

"There he goes!" one of the men yelled.

Gaucho didn't stop to see if they were closing in. He ran as fast as he could—his chest pounding with fear, his breath coming hard and loud.

"Oh, God! Help me, help me," he moaned.

He ran past the florist and the subway entrance. Where was Blanco? Where was the car?

Gaucho glanced behind him quickly. The men in the coats were in close pursuit. Gaucho dashed across the street, narrowly missing being struck by a taxi. An angry bus driver punched his horn. "Crazy kid! Watch where you're going," he yelled, leaning out the window.

Gaucho darted through the heavy traffic. He could hear loud voices behind him.

The large crowd of Chinese pedestrians paid little attention to the chase. Gaucho pushed and squeezed his body through the mob, hurrying toward warm places. The cold air stung his face and tears slid down his cheeks.

Then Gaucho spotted a dark, narrow alleyway. He

glanced over his shoulder and caught sight of his pursuers as they towered over the smaller Chinese people. Gaucho sprang down the alley, his hands touching the brick wall for support as he slid on the cobblestones. His legs were numb except for a throbbing pain shooting up from one of his knees.

Gaucho reached the end of the alley just as the men in the suits appeared, outlined beneath the pink and green flashes of a neon sign. Gaucho hit the pavement and squeezed himself against the building. From where he was lying he could see the men at the open end of the alley bouncing up and down . . . turning . . . searching. . . . He saw one of them speak into a walkie-talkie. They were cops! Had to be.

A new fear gripped him. His mind raced to Benny and the night he died on the roof. He could see the cops and the stretcher, the men in the white uniforms . . . he could hear Benny's mother screaming in disbelief. What if these cops found him? What if they thought he had a gun? What if they made a mistake—like with Benny—and shot him?

Gaucho held on to his throbbing leg. He knew if they came into the alley he'd be found. He couldn't go on. It hurt just to breathe.

The men entered the alley. Gaucho rose to his hands and knees and started crawling quickly, keeping his body pressed against the building. He could feel the bricks snagging on his jacket and heard a rip.

It was getting harder to move. His arms ached. His leg was stiffening. Every motion brought on a new wave of pain. His hands scraped against the sidewalk as he pushed his weight along on his palms.

He could hear the voices behind him in pursuit. It was only a matter of time. . . .

Gaucho came to the end of the alleyway and rounded the corner. He glanced behind him and saw the men drawing nearer. Gaucho leaped to his feet and started running. It took every last ounce of strength he had.

He ran down the block like a madman, knocking over garbage cans, bumping into people. They wouldn't get him without a fight.

"Hey! Gaucho! Get in!" He heard Blanco's voice. It sounded scared. Gaucho looked up and saw the black car alongside him. Blanco threw open the door.

The car was still moving. Gaucho jumped on the hood, bounced off the fender, scampered to his feet, and ran alongside.

Blanco reached over as far as he could. "Give me your hand! Come on!"

Gaucho leaned in and Blanco yanked him hard. Gaucho landed on the front seat and crouched down out of sight. Blanco reached over and closed the door.

"Stay down till I tell you," Blanco said, as he steered the car easily through the narrow streets. He was careful to stop for every red light and stop sign. He even waited patiently while a woman with a loaded shopping cart made her way across the street.

Once safely out of Chinatown, the car picked up speed as they traveled through the deserted waterfront area.

"You can come up now," Blanco said, lighting a cigarette.

Gaucho didn't hear him. He was crying. His sobs came in loud spasms. He couldn't stop. His hands were still trembling. His whole body was cold. His leg throbbed like a steady heartbeat.

"It's okay. It's okay." He felt Blanco's hand on his hair. "Come on. Sit up here." His voice was gentle.

Gaucho moved slowly, hoping to avoid more pain—and then he noticed that his fingers were still gripping the shopping bag!

He jumped up on the seat and left the bag on the floor. For that paper bag he had almost been killed!

"You did good. You did real good."

Gaucho wiped his eyes with his wrist. His body was too weary—too achy—for him to cry anymore.

He leaned back against the seat and wondered if he'd ever see his mother again.

13

A ghost, a ballerina, a clown, and a fat lady with balloons for a chest knocked on the door.

"*Entra. Entra,*" Pachecko called out cheerfully. He pretended to be frightened by the ghost, which amused the ghost and his friends.

Mama greeted the children and led them to the living room, where an assorted group of gaily costumed people were crowded around the record player.

"Wait a minute," Pachecko said, eyeing the fat lady with the golden curls, the long silk gown, and the twin balloons under her blouse. "This ugly woman looks like somebody I used to go out with."

Everyone howled. Even Mama laughed.

"I'm not kidding. I used to go out with this ugly girl back home, and we almost got married except she was so ugly that every time we walked down the streets the dogs would bark and the cats would cry. The birds wouldn't sing and even the moon would hide behind the clouds. One time I took her home and she looked at my goldfish. It drowned."

Señora Cabrera giggled. "Sounds like a perfect woman for you."

"She was perfect in every way, except she was so ugly. The reason we didn't get married is 'cause we couldn't find a priest who could look at her without laughing."

Mama sighed and shook her head. She walked to the window and, as she'd been doing all night, opened it and leaned out.

"You sure you not a relative of that sweetheart of mine?" he asked the fat lady.

"Positive," squeaked Mario, putting a chubby hand on his hip. The other hand held a black lace fan which he flickered in front of his face, concealing all but his mischievous eyes. "All the people in my family are beautiful."

"So what happened to you?" Pachecko roared.

"I'm beautiful inside," Mario said, drawing himself tall with pride. "And outside I'm rich."

Pachecko lit his cigar from the pilot light on the stove. "If I was you," he puffed, his belly leaning against the top of the stove, "I wouldn't go outside till my outside got pretty. 'Cause, woman . . . you sure is ugly!"

Mario wiggled out of the room amid a chorus of laughs. He paused at the living room doorway and said, "You ain't so hot yourself."

Everyone cheered, and Mario joined in with the rest

of his friends bobbing for apples with their teeth from a tub of water.

Then it finally occurred to him. He sat up, looked around the room, and dashed into the kitchen, almost tripping on his long skirt.

"Hey, where's Gaucho?"

"Right here!" Gaucho smiled as he burst into the room.

"Gauchito!" Mama rushed to his side and hugged him close. "Gauchito, I was so worried." She squeezed his face between her hands.

Gaucho grinned, trying to conceal the pain that shot through his body.

"Where were you, *hombre?*" asked Pachecko. His gaze quickly took in Gaucho's soiled hands and face, his torn jacket, and the way he held his leg stiffly.

"I had to do a favor for a friend," Gaucho said, heading for his room.

"What friend? What kind of favor? You look like you were in a fight," Mama said, following him into the room. "How come you didn't call me right away? You know you're supposed to come right home from work. You didn't tell me nothing about going to some friend's house." She stood glaring at him.

"Mama, it was a customer. He came into the store just when I was leaving, and he said he'd pay me if I helped him move furniture to his new apartment. I couldn't call you because he didn't have a phone yet. I thought he only had a little bit of stuff but it was a lot. We just got finished," he said, sitting on his bed.

His heart was pounding. He hoped his voice sounded natural. Looking beyond Mama, Gaucho could see his uncle Pachecko looking at him with a stern expression.

"You know this person?"

"Yeah. He comes into the store a lot. He knows you. He always says to say hello. I don't know his name, but if you saw him, you'd know him."

"The next time you see him, you show him to me because I'm going to tell that man a few things. He has no right to ask a young boy to do such heavy work and send him home like this. Why didn't he come upstairs with you? Ha! What kind of friend is this that sends you home like that!"

Pachecko put his arm on Mama's shoulder. "The boy is home and he's safe and he's all right. Tomorrow is plenty of time. Right now he has all his friends here."

Mama sighed. She allowed her anger to subside. *"Sí,"* she agreed. She waved her finger in Gaucho's face. "Never do that again."

"Don't worry. I won't."

"All right." She smiled. "Get dressed and come to the party." She pulled the curtain closed behind her.

"Mama," he called after her. "Bring me a towel and a wet cloth so I can wash up."

"Okay."

Mama handed him the towels under the hem of the curtain.

Gaucho sat on the edge of his bed and carefully slid off his pants. The material stuck to the dried blood on his knee. He dabbed at the cut with the wet cloth, at the same time pulling on the material. He tensed his body, bit his lip nervously, and gave the pants a strong yank. He winced in pain as the cloth gave way.

"Come on, man." Mario laughed from the other side of the curtain. "You're missing the whole thing."

Drops of perspiration slid down Gaucho's neck. His head pounded and his whole body felt sore.

"I'll be right out," he called, hoping his voice sounded cheerful.

Gaucho slipped into his astronaut costume, which was laid out neatly on top of his dresser. Mama had made the costume from a pair of white woolen pajamas and had stuffed the legs and arms with cotton to make it balloon fully. She had sewn an American flag on the shoulder and made the wide white belt out of braided material. For boots, Gaucho wore her white galoshes, which Angel had given her one Christmas, and on his hands were thick white cotton worker's gloves that he had borrowed from Mario's father.

However, the best part of the costume was the white motorcycle helmet with the blue-tinted sun visor and plastic face protector that snapped shut across his face.

He had taken money out of his secret fund to buy the helmet, but it was worth it.

Gaucho took the white circle of rope from the top of the dresser and pinned it to his waistband.

He stood in front of the mirror and compared his image with that of the small picture he had clipped out of the newspaper showing an astronaut walking to his capsule. Gaucho smiled, and all his pain and anxiety slipped away. He had the best, smartest mother in the whole world.

Gaucho flung aside the curtain and was greeted by cheers and applause.

"Look at that," Señora Cabrera gasped. "Maria! You made that? All by yourself? It's beautiful."

"Son of a gun." Pachecko whistled. "What happened to my skinny nephew who went into that room? Where this fat man come from?" he asked Mama.

Then Pachecko started laughing. "Hey, Mr. Astronut, come here. I got a girlfriend for you," he said, leading Gaucho into the living room by his rope.

"There." He led Gaucho up to Mario. "Maria. Get the camera!"

Gaucho squinted through his blue visor. He lifted the plastic lid slightly. "Mario?" Gaucho tried to suppress a giggle. "Mario?"

Mario threatened him under his breath. "Don't start nothing."

Gaucho turned away to avoid laughing outright.

"Okay. All you crazy people—or whatever you are—get together," Pachecko said, holding the camera.

"Hey, you—the gorilla!" He pointed at a black, hairy costume. "Get next to the banana!"

"I'm no banana," a small, girlish voice squeaked from under the tall, thin, yellow costume. "I'm a sunflower."

"You may be a sunflower in your mind, but to me you are a skinny banana that's going to be eaten by that black gorilla. Now, you stand there like a banana," Pachecko said as he snapped a picture of his own face, the blue flash exploding in his eyes. He dropped the camera and shielded his eyes.

"You okay?" Mama rushed to him.

"Yeah. Yeah." Pachecko smiled, opening and closing his eyes a few times.

Everyone was waiting quietly, not knowing what to say.

"That sure was dumb, *Tio*." Gaucho grinned.

Pachecko threw back his head and laughed. "I may be dumb, but I'm pretty," Pachecko said, puffing on his cigar.

"Here." He handed Mama the camera. "You take the pictures. I go in the kitchen and do the man's work—I'll cut the cake."

For the next three hours, the small apartment shook with the sound of balloons popping, kids laughing, and music blaring.

They ate, threw popcorn at each other, told ghost stories with all the lights out, and screamed in terror when Pachecko tiptoed into the dark room and moaned loudly from underneath a dark blanket.

In their scramble to safety, Mario lost half of his balloon chest.

By 10:30 the last group of parents had come to retrieve their weary and food-swollen children. Everyone went home with some candy, a cup of popcorn, and an apple.

Mario was the last to leave. He waited as Mama wrapped a large chunk of cake for him to take home.

"Gracias." He smiled.

"De nada," Gaucho's mother said, ruffling his hair. The blond wig had long since collapsed and was now hanging near the neckline of Mario's dress. *"Buenas noches,"* she told Mario and his mother.

"Buenas noches, Maria," Señora Cabrera said, kissing her on the cheek.

"Thank you for helping me." Mama patted her arm.

"Thank you." Her friend smiled. "That was the best party I was ever at."

"Good night, Gaucho," Mario called out as he headed wearily upstairs.

Mama closed the door softly. She leaned against it, exhausted.

"Gauchito," she said, walking into the kitchen. "Mario said good night."

She didn't get any response. She looked in Gaucho's room and then stuck her head in the living room.

There, on the couch, stretched out on his uncle's lap, was Gaucho—fast asleep with his helmet resting on his stomach.

Pachecko was slumped against a bunch of throw pillows, his head cradled in his arm, which rested against a bag of potato chips. An empty beer can rested near his thigh, and the dark stump of the cigar dangled from his lip.

He, too, was fast asleep.

14

Gaucho woke up the next morning in his own bed. The first thing he saw was his white helmet on top of the dresser. He smiled. So what if the gorilla won? Everyone knew that kindhearted Pachecko was partial to animals. At least Gaucho had a new shiny helmet and—

Suddenly he remembered! Blanco! Gaucho bolted upright and grabbed his leg in pain. He looked down. It was bandaged from his ankle to the top of his knee. He could see by the thickness of the skin surrounding the bandage that his leg had started to swell. Gaucho saw that he was wearing just his pajama top and shorts. Mama must have undressed him and tended his leg. He had slept through it all.

"Mama. Mama," he called, leaning on his elbows.

He heard quick footsteps and saw his curtain slide open.

"Hi," Jimmy Raddigan stuck in his head. "Your

mother went upstairs for a minute to borrow something. She'll be right back. How you doing?" He smiled.

"Okay." Gaucho was nervous. Why was *he* here? Did he find out about yesterday?

"How's the leg?" Jimmy asked.

"Okay," Gaucho lied. He pulled the blanket across his body. "Hey! What time is it? I'll be late for school."

"Just take it easy. You're not going to school today," Jimmy said, sitting on the edge of the bed.

Gaucho's heart pounded. He did know! He thought of the money lying under his bed. Maybe Mama had found it.

"Jimmy?" he heard his mother call.

"In here. With Gaucho."

Mama rushed into the room. "How's my baby?" She held his face and kissed it. "You okay? The leg hurt?"

Gaucho tried to move it. It was too painful. "Yeah. I'm fine," he said, but his knee throbbed.

"How did you do that to your leg? When I saw it last night I almost fainted. I put on the bandages and washed it. You were so tired you never woke up. I didn't get no sleep. I sat in the kitchen all night in case you woke up and needed something," she said, stroking his arm.

Gaucho felt sorry for her. She looked very tired. Her eyes were dull and her face was sort of gray. Deep circles ringed her eyes.

"I fell when we were moving the furniture. I fell down

the stairs." Gaucho breathed deeply and prayed silently for the pain to go away.

"I think we better go," Jimmy said firmly. "Right now."

"Where?" Gaucho's eyes expanded with fear. "Where we going?"

Mama smiled. "Don't get excited." She began taking some clothes out of the dresser.

"I'll go downstairs and start up the car so it'll be warm. Then I'll come up and get you," Jimmy said, putting on his thick red hunting jacket. He wore a white woolen cap with sunglasses pushed up on the rim. He looked more like a skier than a cop.

"Be right back," he said, and quickly left.

Gaucho's voice came out in small nervous spurts. "Mama. What . . . what is going on?"

"Nothing, *hijo,* we just taking you to the doctor to have him check your leg," she said as she slid off his pajama top and dressed him in a heavy sweatshirt and sweater. "I saw last night how bad the leg looked and all night in your sleep you were crying. I sat in the kitchen all night, I was so worried."

Gaucho's heart thumped. He had dreamed about the chase and the old Chinese woman. He had run down the same narrow streets, fearing for his life. No wonder he had cried. What if he had talked aloud?

"This morning I saw it was all swollen so I called Angel right away, but Denise said he was sleeping and

133

said I couldn't talk to him. She was going out so I couldn't talk to her, but Jimmy was there and thank God she gave him the phone, so he came right away. He took the day off from work just for this and we're not going to the clinic. He's going to take us to a real doctor's office," Mama said. She brushed back Gaucho's hair from his forehead. "He even called the doctor and told him we were coming." She smiled. "He's a wonderful person, Jimmy."

Gaucho wondered how wonderful Jimmy the cop would be if he knew how Gaucho really hurt his leg.

Mama held out his dungarees. "Can you move the leg?"

Gaucho pulled off the cover and tried. He winced and fell back in pain. "No, Mama. It hurts too much."

"What are we going to do? You can't go outside without clothes on."

"The car's heating up," Jimmy said as he came into the room. "We ready?"

Mama explained the problem of dressing Gaucho.

"Does he have a bathrobe?"

Mama nodded. *"Si,* I get it." Together, gently holding him and supporting him, they maneuvered his arms into the bathrobe.

"Okay, champ," Jimmy said, wrapping him in the heavy blanket. "You ready?"

Gaucho nodded. He didn't know what he was supposed to be ready for, but he figured it was safer agreeing.

"Okay." Jimmy leaned over. "Put your arms around my neck, hold on tight, and I'll lift you."

"You mean you gonna carry me? Like a baby!" Gaucho was humiliated.

"Unless you think you can walk to the car."

"Sure I can!" Gaucho whipped off the blanket, turned his body, and cried out, "Mama!"

"I know, my baby. I know." She kissed his head. "You be all right soon."

"Come on, fella, grab on." Jimmy grinned. "Grit your teeth. When I count three I'll slide my arm under you and pick you up. Ready?"

Gaucho nodded. What was the use protesting? There was no way he was going to walk by himself.

"One, two, three!" Jimmy hoisted him high into his arms. "Wrap the blankets around him. It's cold out there," Jimmy told Mama.

Mama wrapped the edges of the blanket around his feet. "Okay." She quickly threw on her coat.

"Where's your hat?" Jimmy asked.

"I never wear a hat," Mama said. "I don't like hats."

"No hat, we don't go. You can't go outside in cold weather without a hat."

Mama looked at him sternly. "My hair is long. It keeps me warm."

"Nope."

Mama could see he wasn't kidding. "But I have no hat. What you want me to do? I never had a hat in my life. Back home nobody wears them except to keep out the sun and even then I never wear a hat."

Jimmy sighed. "Gaucho. Take off my hat and give it to her."

Gaucho slid off the wool ski hat and handed it to Mama. She hesitated.

"Listen, Mama, I'm standing here holding a hundred pounds and the longer it takes you to make up your mind . . . Meanwhile, this boy is in pain. . . ."

That did it! Mama pushed the hat on her head and stomped out of the apartment. Gaucho and Jimmy looked at each other and chuckled silently. Mama was mad as hell!

As they were going down the stairs, Mama marching ahead and Jimmy carrying Gaucho, the Rivera family was coming up the stairs lugging their rolled-up rug, the television, the toaster oven, the new leather bar, and two stools.

"It's the first of the month," Señora Rivera explained meekly. Her sons gladly paused to put down their load.

"That's too bad," Mama snapped. She walked down the stairs and out of the building.

"What's the matter with her?" asked the woman.

"Gaucho's not feeling well and she's worried. But he'll

be okay," Jimmy said as he maneuvered Gaucho's extended stiff leg down the narrow staircase.

"*Dios mio!*" The woman quickly blessed herself. "Poor Gauchito. Get well, my baby." She blew a kiss as she watched them go down the stairs. "Okay, boys, up!" she told her sons. "We just put the stuff on the roof."

Her sons groaned and lifted the furniture.

Outside on the sidewalk, Mama got into the car first and opened the door wide. Jimmy gently and carefully deposited Gaucho onto her lap.

Mama happily assumed the burden.

"That's a lot of kid," Jimmy said, getting behind the wheel. Gaucho glanced over at him and laughed. Then he smiled.

Jimmy pulled away from the curb and into traffic. Gaucho continued to smile. It had been a long time since he'd been held in Mama's arms. He stole another glance at Jimmy—who caught it and winked at him.

Gaucho winked back.

The leg hardly hurt at all.

"I think you'll like Dr. Peterson," said Jimmy as he carried Gaucho into the waiting room. "He's been our family doctor since I was a baby."

Jimmy sat Gaucho on the leather couch and tucked the blanket snugly under his legs as the blond receptionist looked on with amusement.

"Who's your cute friend?" she asked.

Gaucho turned his head in disgust. Here he was in a crowded waiting room with strangers staring at him, dressed in a bathrobe and wrapped up like a baby. And now this silly woman was flirting with him.

"What happened to you?" She smiled at Gaucho. "You fall off a horse?"

Everyone in the waiting room laughed. Gaucho felt uncomfortable.

A man got up and gave Mama his seat. *"Gracias."* She nodded. She looked about the bright, cheerful room with the paintings on the wall, the real plants in the window, and the soft, melodic music seeping overhead.

It was the first time she'd been in a doctor's office in America. Whenever Angel or Gaucho had gotten sick, she had taken them to the neighborhood clinic, or if it was serious or at night, she would take them to the emergency room of the hospital. Private doctors were for rich people.

"You can go in now," the nurse told Jimmy as she pushed a wheelchair next to Gaucho. "Get in, honey, I'll take you for a spin." She winked at him.

Gaucho could hear the other patients giggling. He felt his face burning. He glanced at Mama. She was deeply intent watching the fish swim in the large aquarium. He had to smile. Mama looked awfully silly in Jimmy's wool hat.

"Okay, tiger, let's go." The nurse put her arm around him and, with Jimmy's help, lowered Gaucho into the chair.

"Mama!" Gaucho called as the nurse wheeled him out of the waiting room.

"Si, hijo." Mama jumped up, reluctantly taking her eyes from the parade of gliding fish.

"Good to see you, Jim," said Dr. Peterson, extending his hand. "Is this the fellow you called about?" he asked, standing in front of the wheelchair, his arms folded across his long white coat.

"Yes, sir," Jimmy answered. "I'd like you to meet Mrs. Maria Campos, and this is her son, Gaucho."

The doctor extended his hand to Mama. "How do you do, Mrs. Campos?"

Mama found it hard to speak. She managed a weak smile. It was the first time ever that a doctor had called her by name.

By the time she left the office half an hour later, she and the doctor and the receptionist were chatting as if they were old friends. Gaucho had been examined, X-rayed, and his leg unbandaged and rebandaged.

"Your mother should have been a nurse," he told Gaucho. "She did an excellent job of treating the injury, and there's nothing that I can add to her prescription. Just stay off the leg till the swelling goes down, soak the leg, and change the bandage when it needs it."

The doctor wrote a prescription for a painkiller and also a note for the school nurse. "I want him home for at least a week, and bring him back to me in two weeks."

"I will," Mama told him.

Mama thanked him, Jimmy wrote out a check, and they left, but not before Mama said good-bye to the fish by tapping on the glass tank.

"Put your hat on," Jimmy whispered as he carried Gaucho outside.

Mama pulled the hat down over her ears without so much as a word.

Jimmy spent the rest of the day in the apartment with Mama and Gaucho. For dinner he went out and bought a large pizza, salad for three, and garlic bread and, for dessert, cherry Italian ice. After they ate, he and Gaucho sat at the kitchen table playing checkers while Mama embroidered a pillow case.

Suddenly, Mario burst in without knocking to announce that Blanco had been shot.

15

"What?" Gaucho cried.

"It's on television," Mario gushed; then he recognized Jimmy and froze. He hadn't known him immediately because he wasn't wearing a uniform. Mario flashed Gaucho a look of anguish.

Mama moved quickly and turned on the television. Right after the commercial, the newscaster told of a shootout between police and "a young man believed to be linked to various underground activities, including a counterfeiting operation."

A picture of Blanco flashed on the screen as the newscaster told of police breaking into his apartment after a woman accomplice was arrested in Chinatown. Blanco was shot as he resisted arrest. An officer was also wounded.

"Police uncovered a series of engraving plates and an undetermined amount of counterfeit money. Detectives reportedly also discovered an address book, which police are hopeful will lead them to other members of the operation. Meanwhile, the suspect remains in critical condition at Roosevelt Hospital. He is charged with attempted murder, assault with a deadly weapon, and being in the possession of counterfeit money."

The announcer then switched to the weather report.

Gaucho sat stunned. The color drained from his face. What if his name was in that address book?

"Did you know him?" Jimmy asked Mario.

"Yeah." Mario nodded. "Well—I have to go." He ran out of the apartment.

"Did you know him, Gauchito?"

"Sure, Mama." Gaucho cleared his throat. It was suddenly very dry, and he was having trouble getting any sound out. "Everybody knew him."

"Not everybody," Mama snapped. "I didn't know him and I'm glad. Sounds like an animal."

Gaucho heard the words rush out before he could stop them. "That's not true. He's nice. He's—" Gaucho looked around nervously.

"Where did you know him from?" Jimmy asked, still staring at the checkerboard.

"He hung around school a lot," Gaucho said. "Whose move is it? Mine?" He tried to concentrate on the game.

"No, mine," Jimmy said. "What kind of guy is he?"

Gaucho toyed nervously with his checkers. "Oh . . . just nice. Always likes to talk. Buys you a soda."

Jimmy nodded. "I guess he had a lot of money to spend. I mean, he was making it himself." He laughed.

Gaucho also laughed—to be polite.

"Bet he drove a big car and wore terrific clothes, huh?"

Gaucho nodded. "Yeah, like my uncle Pachecko." He wondered why he had said such a dumb thing. He could feel Mama's anger from across the room. She stormed over to his side.

"Your uncle Pachecko is no murderer. No thief! He never stole nothing from nobody and he never hurt nobody. Maybe he does some things that are not right but he is a good man." Then she remembered that Jimmy was in the room and her eyes mirrored her fear.

Jimmy noticed.

"It's all right, Mama," Jimmy told her. "Even cops can tell the difference between a real criminal and someone who . . . someone who sells hope."

Mama's hand flew to her breast. "You mean you—know?"

"Be pretty dumb if I didn't." Jimmy moved his checker across the board and jumped three of Gaucho's men. "Crown me."

"And you not mad?" Mama asked.

"Who could be mad at Pachecko?" Jimmy laughed. "Besides, there's a lot of people today who don't think that numbers is such a terrible crime. In fact, in New Jersey, right across the river, it's legal. The state is in the numbers business. You can walk into any candy store and play a number."

"But he's still wrong to do it," Mama said. "He's my

brother-in-law and I love him, but he's still wrong." She turned to Gaucho. "And I don't want you talking to such people like that one on the television. I catch you—I punish you!"

"Don't worry. Okay?" Gaucho could feel the nervous sweat dripping down his back. "Okay if we quit now?" he asked Jimmy. "I'm tired."

"Sure," Jimmy said, jumping up to help Gaucho. "Want me to carry you in or you gonna hop?"

"I'll hop," said Gaucho, leaning on the table for support.

"Okay. I'll put the game away."

Gaucho made his way into his room. Mama followed and helped him into bed. She leaned down and kissed him good night.

"Gauchito," she whispered, bringing the blanket up to his chest. "I want you to like Jimmy. He cares for you very much. He told me since he was a little boy he always wanted a brother. Now he feels like he has one."

Gaucho didn't like it when she talked so sad.

"Good night, Mama," he told her, and turned on his side to face the wall.

"*Buenas noches, hijo.*" She patted his head and walked out, pulling the curtain shut behind her.

"Good night, Jimmy," Gaucho called.

"Good night, tiger," Jimmy answered.

Gaucho lay in bed and stared at the light patterns on the ceiling from the flickering candle on top of the refrigerator that danced its image overhead.

He listened as Mama and Jimmy talked quietly. They sounded so natural together. So comfortable. He had noticed how much happier Mama had seemed these days.

Tears rolled silently down his face. What if his name was in the book—or Blanco told the police about him? What if the old woman identified him?

Then a new terror struck. What if Mr. Slavin was also involved?

Sure . . . now it all suddenly came together. Of course he was working with Blanco. Slavin taught photography. Darkroom. Chemicals. Paper. That package he had delivered. It was small but heavy. A little larger than the size of a dollar bill but much heavier. Had it been one of those counterfeit plates? Maybe Slavin was running the whole operation from his darkroom. What if the police somehow traced it to Slavin? What if they gave him a break if he told who else was involved?

What if the police went around through the neighborhood talking to people and someone remembered seeing Gaucho sitting with Blanco in the luncheonette?

Then Leon flashed into his mind. Gaucho panicked! The police were always harassing Leon. They knew he was involved in a lot of things. What if they started putting on pressure and he told about Gaucho delivering the envelope?

Gaucho turned his face into the pillow and cried.

"Oh, God, I'm sorry. God, I'm so sorry." He buried his face. "All I wanted to do was go home."

16

In the week that followed, Gaucho stayed in the apartment watching television and playing soldiers with Mario.

Angel came over with Denise one night and brought him a plastic car model to assemble. Gaucho hopped to his dresser and brought out the fancy chrome and silver racer that he and Jimmy had worked on three nights in a row.

Denise was sitting at the table. "You and Jimmy made that?"

"Yep." Gaucho nodded. "He helped me glue it and put the parts in the right place. But I painted it."

"Pretty fancy." Angel smiled, ruffling his hair.

Denise also smiled, but it was a forced smile. Gaucho knew she was upset about something. Mama noticed it too as she placed the coffee cups in front of them.

"Anything wrong?" Mama asked.

"No," said Angel, poking in the refrigerator. "Everything's fine."

"It's just . . ." Denise looked down and stirred her coffee. "Jimmy's been spending a lot of time here and

. . . well . . . my mother's a little upset because he doesn't come over that much. He used to drive her shopping. He used to take her to bingo. Now she hardly ever sees him. And when she does, he has to leave right away to come here for dinner or something."

There was a long silence. Mama felt uncomfortable and avoided looking at Denise. Gaucho felt guilty and he didn't know why. Angel looked at Denise coldly.

"Your mother's nothing but a troublemaker," he said, slamming the refrigerator door shut.

"Angel," Mama shouted. "That's no way to talk!"

"Well, it's true. The woman does nothing but complain day and night. If it's not one thing, it's something else. I don't even bother talking to her unless I have to."

Denise was steaming. Gaucho could see her knuckles turn white as she gripped the end of the table.

"This is no place to discuss our business," Denise said.

"This is my home. I can discuss anything I want here. We're not in your mother's house now where she's always listening. Always asking questions." He pulled the chair roughly away from the table and sat down. "We're getting our own place, away from her, as soon as that baby is born."

Mama screamed. "What? What? Angel! A baby?"

"Yes, Mama." He jumped up and hugged her. "There's going to be a baby."

Soon everyone was laughing and crying and kissing each other. Even Gaucho was caught up in the emotion.

"I'm gonna be an uncle?" His eyes shone.

"You sure are. Every Saturday you'll have to take him to the movies and the park and teach him all the dirty words you know." Angel laughed.

"Why didn't you tell us?" Mama said as she hugged Denise.

"We wanted to wait till we were sure. Now we are. That's why I went to the doctor the other day when you called. I was nervous. I should've talked to you longer, but. . . ." She lowered her eyes. "I'm sorry . . . Mama."

Mama smiled through her tears. "That's okay." Then she excused herself and went into the living room.

The brothers knew that Mama was in the other room saying a silent prayer of thanks and safekeeping. They had been through this many times, whenever there was good news—or bad news—to share.

Angel threw his arm around Gaucho's shoulder. "As soon as the baby is born, we're getting a little apartment of our own. Maybe even around here, so you can come up after school. You gonna be his only uncle on our side of the family, and that's an important thing to be," he said.

Gaucho nodded and thought warmly of his uncle Pachecko. It *was* an important person to be.

"What if it's a girl?" asked Gaucho.

"Girls need uncles too. Maybe more. Especially ones who know how to put things together," he said, admiring the silver chrome sports car.

Gaucho felt proud. He looked at Denise. He wondered if they would ever be friends. Then he supposed they would. After all, she was Jimmy's sister.

His first day back in school. Gaucho was treated like a returning hero. He used fancy crutches that Jimmy had borrowed from the first-aid room at the precinct. He hadn't seen most of his friends since the Halloween party, and there was a lot to catch up on.

Even the teachers were unusually pleasant to him, he felt. They took extra care to explain to Gaucho the work he had missed. They fussed over him and helped him store his crutches in the cloakroom along with his coat. Even the principal had a friendly greeting when Gaucho hobbled toward him in the hall.

Gaucho found it hard to remain humble.

During lunch in the cafeteria, his friends brought him his food tray from the counter and surrounded him as he ate, catching him up on all the latest gossip.

"I guess you heard about Mr. Slavin," one of the girls said.

Gaucho dropped his fork. "No! What!"

"Oh, yeah, he moved to Florida. We have a new science teacher. Real creep. She thinks she knows everything."

Gaucho casually sucked the straw in his milk container. He hoped he looked and sounded disinterested. "That right? He . . . just left?"

"Took off. I heard he was getting a divorce or something. I heard the secretaries in the office talking about it. They were mad, 'cause he just quit without telling them and they had to hire somebody else right away."

Gaucho breathed easily. He had been dreading having to confront Mr. Slavin. Whatever his connection with Blanco had been, it couldn't have been too serious if he wasn't arrested.

Eventually the topic got around to Blanco.

"You used to be a friend of his, huh, Gaucho?" somebody asked.

Gaucho nodded. "Yeah. I knew him."

"Too bad he died," one of the girls said.

Gaucho looked down at his tray and, like Mama, said a silent prayer. For his friend.

On their way home from school, he and Mario stopped at Armando's store.

"When you coming back to work?" asked the owner.

"I have to go to the doctor at the end of the week, and I'll ask him and see what he says."

"Well, I'll hold your job. You know that. Try to get back soon, 'cause the people been asking for you. Okay?"

"Okay." Gaucho waved as he and Mario left the store.

Gaucho and Mario hurried home, bent against the cold, icy wind. Mario held all the books while Gaucho maneuvered his crutches.

Glancing down the block at the park, Gaucho could see the clumps of yellow and orange and red leaves atop the thinning skeletons of trees. Soon it would be winter, and with it snow and rides down the hill on large pieces of cardboard. They would build a fort and throw snow-balls at buses.

At night, when it was dark and still, he and Mama would go to the store on some pretext—like buying a newspaper—and then walk the long way home so they could tramp on the fresh snow and carry pieces of it home on their boots and gloves.

There was something about walking on snow at night with no one else around that just had to be the best thing in the world to do.

Gaucho noticed that the store windows were advertising plump turkeys. One store had a large pyramid made of cans of cranberry sauce.

"Smells like snow," Gaucho told Mario.

"Naw. Too early. Never snows before Thanksgiving."

"Maybe this year it'll be different."

"Maybe." Mario shifted the weight of the books. "We going to the parade this year?"

"Sure. If you want to."

Mario laughed. "You know they don't celebrate Thanksgiving in Puerto Rico."

"How come?" Gaucho asked, surprised.

"It ain't their holiday. This is the only place that celebrates it. Teacher told us."

Gaucho thought about it. "Damn. They don't get the four days off?"

"Nope." Mario puffed as they climbed the stairs to

Gaucho's apartment. "We got a letter from there the other day. My mother's cousin said her son cut his foot swimming. Can you imagine swimming this time of year?"

"Down there it isn't this time of year."

"That's right!" Mario said, opening the door for Gaucho. "Down there, every day is the same. That same lousy sun is always shining. You always know tomorrow is going to be the same as today. They can keep it!" Mario said, depositing Gaucho's books on his bed.

"Hello, Mario. Thank you for helping Gaucho," Mama said as she stirred the food on the stove.

"That's okay." He waved. "See ya later. We'll do the homework in the basement," he called to Gaucho.

"Okay."

The kitchen was warm and cozy. The many pots of food steaming spelled company. Mama never cooked that much just for two people.

"*Tio* Pachecko's coming to dinner," she said. "We're having yellow rice and chicken."

Gaucho stretched out on his bed, carefully placing the crutches on the floor.

"Did you notice the sky?" Mama called over her shoulder. "It looks like snow."

"Yeah. I noticed," Gaucho said. Then he added, cheerfully, "Pretty soon."

"Oh, Jimmy stopped by before and he's taking us to the movies tomorrow. He said you can invite Mario if you want."

Gaucho didn't answer. He lay on his bed with his

head resting on his arm and stared at the wall. He wondered if Mr. Slavin would be happy in Florida and hoped that he would be. He wondered what would happen to the old woman.

He fell asleep thinking how precious his home was to him and how close he had come to losing it all.

"Wake up, *hombre*. Time to eat!" Gaucho turned on his side and collided with Pachecko, who was leaning over the bed. "This going to school must be pretty rough stuff." The man laughed. "When I was your age, I cut sugarcane in the fields in the hot sun fourteen hours a day—with only some coffee and bread and butter and maybe a banana to eat the whole day. Fourteen hours under that miserable sun. And you know what I did when I got home?"

Gaucho smiled. "Went to sleep!"

"Like hell!" Pachecko roared. "I went dancing. Me and my ugly girlfriend. The one I told you about. What she didn't have in the face—she had in her feet. That woman could dance!"

Mama could be heard rattling the dishes.

Gaucho pulled himself up to a sitting position and swung his leg over the bed.

"Before you know it, you be dancing. Come on. Let's eat."

"*Tio.*" Something about the sound of Gaucho's voice made Pachecko stop. He turned and looked down at the boy.

"What is it?"

Gaucho stared at the floor. *"Tio.* Did you ever do something really bad in your life? I mean . . . something you could get into a lot of trouble for if someone found out. But . . . I mean . . . it wasn't something you knew was wrong when you did it. I mean . . . maybe I did know in the back of my mind that I was doing something wrong . . . but . . . you see, *Tio* . . . I had a reason." Gaucho couldn't look at his uncle.

He felt Pachecko's weight press down on the bed next to him.

"Hijo," the man said softly. "In this life we do many things. Some are good. Some are bad. Most of these things nobody knows but ourselves. Every person has many, many secrets. Most of them are not happy ones. But . . . things happen in life and a lot of it is bad, that's true, but you can't think of just that because then you might as well give up and be dead. You got to think of the good things, and there are many more good things in this life than we know. Like anything else, if you want to find them, you have to look for them."

He placed his heavy hand on Gaucho's knee. "I done many things I am not proud of, but the one thing I would never do is hurt someone—on purpose. If this thing you did would hurt your mama if she found out—and if it's too late to change what you did—then I say you have to keep it to yourself." He sighed and shook his head. "And that, *hijo,* is the worst punishment in life. Nobody can hurt you as much as you can hurt yourself."

Gaucho understood. He knew the rest of his life he would carry his secret. Alone.

"*Tio*. Is it fun to be an uncle?"

"Sometimes. Why?"

Gaucho shrugged. "I don't know. You do a lot for me, but what do I do for you?"

Pachecko looked at the ceiling. "That's true. I never thought about it. You got the best part of the deal." He laughed.

"I'm gonna be an uncle," Gaucho said, getting up slowly. Pachecko handed him his crutches. "I'm gonna be a good uncle, too."

"The secret to being a good uncle is make plenty of money and spend it just as fast. Come on. I can smell that chicken." He held the curtain open as Gaucho hobbled into the kitchen.

As they sat down to eat, Mario dashed into the room. "Hurry up, Gaucho. I gotta write a report on space travel. I'll meet you down by the washing machines." He ran out.

"I don't know nothing about space travel," Gaucho moaned. "Just 'cause I got a space costume he thinks I know something." Gaucho shook his head and attacked the yellow rice. "That guy sure is dumb."

Mama smiled. It was nice to see Gaucho with a real appetite again. He had seemed so . . . distant lately. Almost as if he were in a daze. She watched happily as he speared the chicken with one hand, reaching with the other for a piece of buttered bread, scooping up the rice on his fork.

"Eats just like his papa," Pachecko observed.

Later that night, after he had helped Mario write his composition, after he had said good-bye to his uncle, long after his mother had fallen asleep on the couch watching television, Gaucho brought the candle from the refrigerator and placed it on the floor near his bed.

He crawled under the bed and got the coffee can. He opened the lid and counted out the money. There was $41.89. Blanco had never paid him for that terrible night, and Gaucho was glad.

Gaucho looked at the money. He smoothed out the wrinkled bills and laid them flat. He put the change in neat piles.

As he sat on the floor, putting the money into his empty cigar box, he wondered if they still had that red tricycle in the window around the corner.

Tricycles didn't care if they were ridden by a boy or a girl.

Maybe there would be enough left over to buy a small aquarium. Nothing too fancy. Just a glass tank, maybe with some plants, and a few fish. Maybe one of those pumps that made the water bubble and a Ferris wheel that rotated like the one in the doctor's office.

Gaucho reached for his box of comics and sat on the floor reading by the light of the flickering candle.